Rachel Mason is in the fifth grade. She is nice. She is pretty. But mostly, she is smart. The other kids know she's smart. Her teacher knows she's smart. But even her teacher doesn't know how smart she really is.

Rachel has lots of nice friends. She has a love for reading and a talent for writing. She even has a dream to grow up and be a teacher someday. But Rachel has something else… a secret. And she is smart enough to keep *this* secret to herself…

Sometimes teachers can recognize problems in a student's life, but some people are good at hiding problems. This was Rachel's special talent – to keep a secret, even a bad one. When a heartbreaking incident jeopardizes her secret as well as her academic success, Rachel faces her toughest challenge yet.

Readers will recognize someone they know – maybe even themselves – when they read Rachel's story.

Rachel Mason

Hears the Sound

by
Cindy Lovell Oliver

Cover art by Marcelle Gilkerson

Lyrics to "That's What Living is to Me" © 1988 and "Growing Older But Not Up" © 1981 by Jimmy Buffett (Used with Permission)

With a foreword by Nathan Levy, Educational Consultant, Author of *Stories with Holes*

N.L. Associates, Inc.
PO Box 1199
Hightstown, NJ 08520-0399

ISBN 1-878347-61-6
Copyright © 2005 N.L. Associates, Inc.

Printed in the United States of America

This book is dedicated to Scotty Tate who always asked, "Neen, why don't you write a book?" to Angie, who is always writing a book, and to Adam, who is always reading a book.

⌘

Special thanks to Emily Tichenor for being my first editor.

Foreword

As an educator I was constantly searching for novels that students could joyously read and study. I wanted to do concentrated studies of books that were of high interest, and superior literary quality. Of course, I also wanted books that children and adults could share in school and at home. *Rachel Mason Hears the Sound* is that kind of book.

Our company publishes activity books for educators and parents to use with children. We have chosen Rachel Mason as our first novel because of its far reaching appeal. The content is extremely relevant to so many readers, and the character immediately gripped our staff. Cindy Oliver has brought a gifted young lady to life that all of us should meet. I loved "meeting" Rachel Mason. I know you will too.

Nathan Levy

Table of Contents

Chapter 1 – Hunger Pains

"All right," Mrs. Juarez called above the din of the classroom, "what did you have for breakfast this morning?" I cringed at the pang in my stomach and distracted myself by listening to the responses.

"The usual," yelled Ronald, "a Barf McMuffin." A couple kids groaned, but Mrs. Juarez just ignored him. She always ignored kids who called out. Several kids were waving their hands in the air or whispering to each other what they had. I overheard a remark about some new kind of berry bagel that sounded good and wished I would have had something like that.

Mrs. Juarez eyed the wavers and finally zeroed in on Elizabeth who hadn't wiggled out of her seat yet.

"Elizabeth, what did you have for breakfast?"

"Captain Crunch," Elizabeth replied sweetly. Elizabeth was a little shy, so an easy question like this was a sure way to get her to raise her hand.

"Good, good. I like Captain Crunch with crunch berries," replied Mrs. Juarez, smiling her excited smile, the one she wore when everyone was paying attention, or when all the students were on their best behavior. "Let's see, who else… Jonathan, what did you have for breakfast?" Jonathan smiled triumphantly.

"My mom didn't make breakfast. We stopped at the Quick Stop, and I bought this donut for snack time!" He took the donut from his desk and held it up, waving it back and forth like it was some kind of prize on a TV game show. Two boys lunged for it, but he shoved it back in his desk, laughing. Mrs. Juarez took a little breath and went on.

Around the room she went, nodding and smiling as kids chimed in about what they had or didn't have for breakfast that morning. Leftover pizza, a Tastykake, Mountain Dew, Eggos, nothing… Pretty soon she came to me. In an edgy, desperate voice she asked, "Rachel, what did *you* have for breakfast?" Without batting an eye I gave it to her straight:

"Scrambled eggs, whole wheat toast, and fresh squeezed orange juice." Her eyes lit up like I was the rescue squad and she'd been wandering around without food or shelter.

"Scrambled eggs, whole wheat toast, and fresh squeezed orange juice," she repeated. "That's excellent, Rachel. In case you've all been wondering why I've been asking about your breakfast, it's because today we are going to begin our unit on nutrition. You've all given some *wonderful* examples, and Rachel's breakfast will launch our discussion of the food pyramid."

She unveiled a giant poster of the food pyramid – a bigger version of the one you see on bread wrappers or soup labels – and she was off and running. Mrs. Juarez was a great teacher. She really liked teaching and was always telling us her "methods" and "strategies." For instance, it was no secret to her students that our little breakfast discussion was really her "motivational hook." She always initiated an attention-getting discussion, and then she could proceed with her lesson. I really get a kick out of her. In fact, I know I want to be a teacher when I grow up, so I usually pay more attention to Mrs. Juarez's methods and strategies than I do to her lessons.

"That's right, Kacey, three to five servings of fruit each day," Mrs. Juarez nodded in response to something Kacey had said. I had been in La La Land, but it usually only took me a second or two to find my place again. "So," Mrs. Juarez continued, "why was Rachel's example so useful for this discussion?" Five or six hands went up. It was fun to watch Mrs. Juarez operate. She told us she always tried to ask the question and *then* she would call on a student by name. This way, she said, all our brains were turned "ON" in anticipation of being called on. She looked around at the hands, did a quick mental calculation to see who *hadn't* been called on yet.

"Kenny?" This was Kenny's cue to synthesize what he'd learned so far about the food pyramid. Instead, he just sighed and looked like a deer caught in the headlights. Mrs. Juarez was undaunted. "Rachel had fresh squeezed orange juice," she smiled at Kenny. "Where would we find that on the food pyramid?" This bite-size approach was just what Kenny needed. He looked up at the chart and read it over like it was a menu, scanning for the 'Beverage' section. Not finding it, he shook his head in frustration. I anticipated Mrs. Juarez's response and was not the least bit surprised when she asked, "Where does orange juice come from?" Revelation! Kenny's eyes opened wide. He bypassed the most recent question and went straight for the original.

"Fruits!" he exclaimed.

"Absolutely!" praised Mrs. Juarez. "Orange juice is made from oranges, so Rachel's fresh squeezed orange juice would go in the 'Fruits' category."

Kenny was happy. Everyone was happy. This was going to be an easy lesson. My stomach growled. It wasn't exactly all this talk about food that was making me hungry, although that wasn't helping matters any. The truth was, I had the *right* answer – scrambled eggs, whole wheat toast, and fresh squeezed orange juice – the kind of answer Mrs.

Juarez was looking for, but the trouble was, I hadn't actually had any breakfast that morning.

Chapter 2 – La La Land

I spent a lot of time in La La Land that morning. Mrs. Juarez had put a sign up on the first day of school that read: **La La Land is closed from 8:00 a.m. until 2:30 p.m.** We all knew about the sign before we got to fifth grade, but Mrs. Juarez explained it to us and our parents on "Meet the Teachers" night before school started.

"Sometimes students daydream, and although this is perfectly understandable, my job is to present them with lessons that are personal, meaningful, and relevant. It is my professional goal to maintain the students' interest, and therefore maintain student motivation." She went on to tell us that kids would be unlikely to waste a lot of time daydreaming in her class since it was bound to be so interesting, so she was "officially closing La La Land" during school hours. The parents were duly impressed with Mrs. Juarez's strategy, and the students were relieved to learn that she had a sense of humor.

But, even though La La Land was supposedly closed, I still managed to sneak in occasionally, as did most of my classmates. This morning, for instance, was one of those times. While the rest of the class discussed 'what constitutes a serving size' and Mrs. Juarez provided sneak previews of upcoming lessons, I had more important matters to contemplate and was unable to concentrate on nutritional issues. Once I heard my name, but it was just Mrs. Juarez referring back to the breakfast discussion. That focused me, though, so I reluctantly withdrew from La La Land and rejoined the discussion. "So, to quickly review the concept of a balanced diet, let's use Rachel's breakfast as our first meal, then we'll have someone describe a balanced lunch and someone else describe a balanced supper..." She scanned the faces making sure everyone was as interested as she was before calling on someone. "Okay, for lunch, who can tell us...Juan?" Disappointed hands went down as Juan responded.

"Well I can tell you what it's NOT. It's NOT what we're having in the cafeteria today!" Everyone laughed, even Mrs. Juarez.

"Well, what would you choose, then?" All this talk of food was making me hungry. I looked at the clock. Good. Only five minutes until DEAR time.

DEAR time is my favorite part of the school day. That's Drop Everything And Read time, and we could read anything we wanted for fifteen minutes — books, magazines, even comics. Also, we were allowed to bring a snack. Mrs. Juarez encouraged us to bring a healthy snack to hold us over until lunch, since we were growing fifth-graders with hearty appetites, but most students brought junk food. Sometimes she had pretzels or something that she shared with kids who forgot a snack. I didn't bring a snack today, but I wasn't too worried. Someone was always trying to get rid of an apple or box of raisins or something.

A few minutes later the nutrition discussion ended, and I curled up under my desk to read *The Adventures of Tom Sawyer.* Mr. Riece, my fourth grade teacher, had read us the whitewashing chapter last year, and ever since then I had wanted to know the whole story. Now I was reading the entire book. It was great! I wished Tom Sawyer and Huckleberry Finn were real people who went to our school, but unfortunately, they weren't. There was no one in my school even remotely like Tom or Huck. Then again, I'm glad my teacher was nothing like Tom Sawyer's teacher. Mrs. Juarez would never hit a student, even if he did tear her favorite book. Mrs. Juarez is simply too kind and caring a person. I believe that everyone who knows her feels comfortable and safe in her presence.

This got me reminiscing about the first week of school when she introduced us to the concept of DEAR time. Mrs. Juarez read too, to set an example, and the book she was reading was the size of an encyclopedia. So, all the students, even the ones whose reading skills were questionable, grabbed big, intellectual-type books with no pictures. They were just trying to impress the teacher, and she must have caught on, because on the third day of school she read *The Napping Tree* and the day after that she read the newspaper. I know that she was sending a message to us students that we should read what we enjoy and not pretend to read something just to make an impression.

I was just getting to the part where Tom and Huck were making plans to go to the graveyard when Alice Lee nudged me. "Rachel, look…" She was holding open a Ziploc bag full of cookies.

"Thanks, Alice Lee!" I whispered as I grabbed a handful. Alice Lee to the rescue! We had known each other since first grade. Her mom always packed great snacks, and she never ate them all. I resumed my reading and munched on Alice Lee's cookies. Lunchtime didn't seem so far away now, and I wished I could go on reading all day. There is nothing like getting lost in a good book to forget about your own troubles. DEAR time for me was a lot like La La Land, but it was okay because we had the teacher's permission.

Chapter 3 – A Good Student

The afternoon flew by. Mrs. Juarez returned our math tests. A couple kids looked miserable, but I got a hundred. The test was on calculating percentages, fairly easy stuff. "Now don't worry if you didn't get a perfect score," Mrs. Juarez was saying, "we'll be calculating percentages in our study of nutrition, so you'll have plenty of opportunities to practice this skill."

"My dad doesn't want to hear how much practice I'll get. He'll just be mad I missed so many," Mark Langdon told her. "Just because he's good at math he thinks I should be. Now he'll be hanging over my shoulder watching my every move until the next test." Poor Mark.

I was lucky. My parents never harassed me about homework or test scores. I suppose if I ever did mess up they would have plenty to say, but for the most part, school was something I didn't have to worry about. In fact, school was the one place where I really didn't have any worries.

My older brother, Josh, who is three years older than me, is practically a genius, so any time I started a new school year with a teacher Josh had had I'd always hear, "Oh, you're Rachel *Mason, Josh* 's sister! Josh was an outstanding student, and I'm sure you will be, too!" And that's how it went for my younger brother, Jeremy and me. Jeremy has Mr. Riece this year, so he's got *two* hard acts to follow. Hey, I'm not Josh, but I'm no slouch.

Sometimes my friends tell me how smart I am, and how they wish they were good at math or reading like me. Actually, that makes me feel really good, but I don't make a big deal out of it. There are times when I feel inadequate, and that my work is not up to par, but it always seems to work out. I like doing well in school, and I want to be a teacher when I grow up.

It's nice to be good at something, and for me it's school. My clothes aren't as new or nice as my girlfriends' clothes, because my family is usually on a tight budget. And as far as what I look like, I'm at least a little above average. So, schoolwork is the one thing I have going for me, which is nice.

Occasionally my teachers ask me to help another student who's having a hard time with something. Depending on who it is, I like that. Take Mark Langdon, for instance. Back in third grade I had to help him with his times tables, and he's always kind of liked me ever since. Not like a boyfriend-girlfriend thing. I don't have a boyfriend. But it's nice to know we're friends, and besides, I'll always get picked for teams. Mark might not be a math whiz, but he's good in sports and is usually the captain of one of the teams when we play kickball or softball.

Sometimes helping another student can backfire, though. Back in second grade I had to help this new girl, Amanda, with her spelling words. She couldn't spell her way out of a paper bag, and nothing I did seemed to help. In fact, Amanda resisted my help and actually resented my efforts. I still don't know why Mrs. Griffith put us together, unless it was because I was always the first one done with spelling and Amanda was always the last. So, Amanda simply hated my guts for being a good speller, and never missed an opportunity to get me in trouble over the most inconsequential events.

For instance, when Mrs. Griffith was going over math that I already knew, I would put another book inside my math book to read while Mrs. Griffith droned on about pyramids and cones and triangles. It was a great trick Josh taught me. There I'd be, enjoying the poems of Shel Silverstein or reading a new Judy Blume book, when all of a sudden I'd hear Amanda's whine, "Mrs. Griffith, Rachel Mason is reading a book that's not her math book." Mrs. Griffith, who *did* acknowledge kids who called out, especially tattletales, would chastise me.

"Rachel, girls need to learn math, too. Now sign in." So I'd have to sign in and lose points, and then I really hated helping Amanda with her spelling. One sure thing about living in Florida, though, is that new kids come, but new kids also go. Amanda reminded me of a sign that hangs in the video store in town – 'All of our customers make us smile – Some when they come in, and some when they leave.' I definitely smiled when Amanda left.

Chapter 4 – My Terrible Secret

I always hate the bus ride home and would prefer walking or riding a bike. Trouble is, we live too far from Manatee Elementary, so Jeremy and I are stuck riding the bus. He doesn't seem to mind and always sits with Ben Rollins, our neighbor who's in his class. I sit with Rebecca Shelton or Haley Bennington. Haley's mom is a big fan of Disney movies and named her after Haley Mills, the actress in *Pollyanna* and *That Darn Cat.* Oh, and Haley's favorite, *The Parent Trap.* Mrs. Bennington spouts dialogue from these movies by heart, and we've watched all the videos during Haley's sleepovers.

Rebecca and Haley got off earlier than I did, so I spent the rest of the ride reading, doing homework, or just thinking. I tend to do a lot of thinking on the way home. I'm always amazed at how Jeremy can just laugh and joke around with Ben, but I guess he's just busy having a good time. I, on the other hand, am thinking about what *might* be going on at home.   I learned a long time ago that it didn't matter what was going on in the morning when you left the house, everything could be completely reversed by the time you got off the bus at 3:15.

Take this morning, for instance. My parents, who are really great people, had been fighting half the night. Granted, all parents fight sometimes, but it's different at our house, and impossible to explain. Most importantly, none of my friends know about the fighting – it's my own terrible secret that I will never tell. When my friends talk about their parents fighting, I just keep quiet and wish my parents argued and fussed the way other parents do. But, it's not that way.

I love my parents. My dad works hard as a building contractor, and he always invites us to the job sites so we can watch the houses as they're built. He's extremely talented and builds beautiful houses, each with a unique stained glass window. That's his trademark – a custom designed stained glass window in a special place in each house, usually facing east to catch the morning sun. No two are alike, yet they are equally beautiful. People call constantly and even ask to go on a waiting list because they want a Mike Mason house. My dad is a lot of fun. He has a great sense of humor and plays games with us. He also takes us on vacation whenever he can spare the time, so we really have some good times.

My mom doesn't actually work at a job, but she does the bookkeeping for my dad and takes care of his phone calls and office duties. She orders supplies, handles the payroll, and helps to keep things on schedule. She also takes care of us – Josh, Jeremy, and yours truly, Rachel Mason. She likes to read a lot – like me – and is a regular at the library. She's also a talented musician, and plays bluegrass music. My mom plays the guitar, fiddle, mandolin, and bass. She played in her dad's band when she was just a kid. Who knows? Maybe she could have been a big star if she had stayed with it, but she really doesn't play much anymore. Besides, she and my dad got married, had us kids, and for as long as I can remember, they have been fighting.

This is the hard part. When I say fighting, I mean with hitting and everything. The yelling and cursing are bad enough, but seeing your dad pound your mom with his fists is the worst feeling in the world. I don't want to give the wrong impression about my dad. It's hard to say how great he is and at the same time tell how he hits my mother, but that is the unbelievable truth. My dad really is a great guy, and all my friends wish their dad could be like him. But they don't know the whole story, and I'm certainly not going to tell it. When my dad drinks, he just goes crazy. He says terrible things and hits my mom, and sometimes she hits back, in self-defense. I can't remember the first fight I ever saw, but like I said, they've been going at it as long as I can remember. Josh can remember more, because he's the oldest.

It usually happens at night. Sometimes when my dad finishes working he goes to the bar with some of his buddies. After that, anything can happen. He might come home just feeling happy and go right to sleep. He might come home and start fighting as soon as he walks through the door. Or, like last night, he might come home and fall asleep, then wake up in the middle of the night and start fighting. That's the worst, because we never know if he's going to sleep through the night or wake everyone up with the fighting, and the suspense can be sickening. There is no sorrier sound in the world than being awakened from a dream to the thud of your mother being thrown into a wall or onto the floor.

He doesn't drink often, but on the nights he does it's always very hard to fall asleep not knowing what may happen. Of course we kids hear the screaming and crashing, and of course we get up and watch. Sometimes we cry and beg them to stop, and once Josh even tried to push my dad away from my mother, but mostly we just huddle together, too afraid to do anything. That expression, *'paralyzed with fear'*, is something I have experienced.

We never talk about it. Ever. I feel ashamed because I don't do anything to stop it, but I get so scared I actually feel weak and incapacitated when they're fighting. It's more than helplessness, and more like hopelessness. When my dad sobers up he is sincerely sorry and ashamed. When he's contrite like that, it's hard to imagine he could ever hurt a fly. Then there's my mom, who doesn't go out much for a few days after a fight. Subdued and ashamed, she waits in the car while one of us kids run into the store if we need milk or something. Once her bruises heal, she'll go back to her normal routine. Of course, this *is* the normal routine.

This morning was bad. I heard a loud thud and her first suppressed scream about three in the morning. By seven it was all over - Dad was drinking coffee and apologizing and getting ready to leave for work. Mom was crying and picking up the pieces of something that was smashed – a lamp, I think. Josh, Jeremy, and I just headed off for the bus stop as though it were a regular kind of day. And that's why I hadn't had any breakfast that morning. Of course, I knew what Mrs. Juarez was wanting someone to say, and there's no way I'd ever tell anyone that *I* was ever sent to school with no breakfast! I couldn't believe the kids who told embarrassing stories about their families! Didn't they care what people thought? I would *never* tell anyone what went on in our home, and neither would my brothers.

C

hapter 5 – Scrounging in the Cupboards

When we got off the bus, Ben asked Jeremy if he wanted to come over. "Uh, not tonight. I'll see you in the morning," Jer replied. Now the two of us walked silently toward our driveway. Everything looked perfectly normal. Anyone walking by would never have suspected the morning's events. Jeremy and I got home about fifteen minutes before Josh. There was always a sense of dread going back in the house after a fight, but also an intense desire to make sure everything was all right.

Mom was on the phone. "Yes, as a matter of fact he finished the estimate this morning. I faxed it in to Bailey's office, so we should have an answer by tomorrow." Good. She sounded like Mom, just getting on with her day. In the kitchen something smelled good. Chili. No, spaghetti! That was a good sign. Spaghetti is Dad's favorite. It always seemed so weird that after these horrendous fights they seemed to go out of their way to pretend it didn't happen and that it would never happen again. It wasn't like Dad would come home with flowers or anything. In fact, after he sobered up and apologized, no one ever talked about it again. I went in the family room where Mom was hanging up the phone. Other than the dark circles under her eyes it was impossible to know she had had a bad night.

"How was your day?" she asked.

"Good," I replied. "We're studying nutrition, so I need to take some food labels in. Do we have anything I can take the label from?"

"Well, look through the cupboards. If you take a label off of a can, just write on it with a marker."

I scrounged through the cupboards looking for labels. Green beans. Boring. Red beets. Gross. Spam. Spam! My mom was probably the only person on the planet who bought Spam, but I have to admit, I like the way she makes it. Still, the kids would laugh me back to the second grade if I showed up with a Spam can. Baked beans. That would cause the wrong kind of jokes. Geez! Didn't we have anything decent in our cupboards? Flour, sugar, Crisco.

Maybe the fridge. Pickles, ketchup, lettuce. Sounds like a Burger King commercial. Eggs, milk, cheese. Too everyday. I wanted something with some zing. Some pizazz. Something no other kid would bring. I looked in the lower cupboards. Captain Crunch. That reminded me of Elizabeth. And Mrs. Juarez, who liked crunch berries. Cranberry Almond Nut Crunch. That had possibilities. Rice Chex. Nah. Then I spied a cake mix. No, it was muffin mix. Lemon Poppy Seed muffin mix – my favorite! I read the nutrition label. It had all the nutrition information listed two ways – as a mix, and once it was prepared. That cracked me up! Like someone would eat muffin mix right out of the box! That was it.

"Mom, can I have the box for the lemon poppy seed muffins?"

"You can if you make them tonight," she called back. Mmmmmm…hot muffins, coming right up! I looked over the label again and wondered if anyone in my family would prefer the lower calorie version – unmixed and unbaked.

Chapter 6 – Trying to Concentrate

Half an hour later a warm, sweet lemony smell was competing with the tangy spaghetti sauce. I *love* to cook, but I especially love baking. My mom has been letting me make stuff for years, and I'm pretty good at it. I tidied up and grabbed my homework while I waited for supper to be ready. Math. I started converting decimals to percentages. Nothing too hard, just a little concentration and I had folded the paper and stuck it back inside the math book.

Bzzzzzzzzzz! The timer – my muffins were ready. Jeremy and Josh appeared out of nowhere, pushing to be the first one there. Wearing oven mitts and barely hanging onto a pan full of muffins, I tried to put them on the counter without burning myself. "Watch out, they're hot!" I yelled, trying to keep them from knocking me over. "You can't have any yet! Mom!!!!"

"Josh! Jeremy! You know better. Don't antagonize your sister!" They didn't hear a word she was saying.

"Aw, come on, Rachel, just give us one and we'll leave you alone," Josh begged. "Mom, can't we just have one? We don't care if they're hot."

"You can all have one after supper," Mom replied, coming into the kitchen with an armload of folded towels. "Here, put these away." She thrust the towels into Josh's arms. They covered half his face. Josh started laughing and mumbling behind the towels, then bumped into Jeremy dumping half the towels on him – on purpose.

"Come on, you can help." Jeremy ducked and tried to avoid Josh, pivoted, and collided with Mom. One second later the towels flew everywhere, and there sat Josh in the middle of the pile, laughing.

I flinched. Mom was not amused. "Can't you just do one simple thing I ask you to do?" she implored, her voice hard and tight, full of disappointment and resignation. Instantly Josh was remorseful, but the damage was done. Mom grabbed the towels and headed down the hallway. We could hear her stifling her sobs.

Josh and Jeremy and I looked at each other. I felt sick in my stomach. We all knew it wasn't really the towels. In fact, the towels were really just a diversion from what was troubling Mom. After this morning's early episode, the four of us waited on pins and needles for Dad to come home from work. Often as not, he would pull repeat performances back to back. You just never knew. That's why she made spaghetti – the sauce could just simmer while we waited for Dad. He was already about a half an hour late.

I hated nights like this. I hated them so much. It was the suspense and dread of another possible fight. The not knowing. My stomach was sick, and the muffins no longer held their appeal. I sat back down at the kitchen table to distract myself with the rest of my homework. Josh and Jeremy were in their bedrooms, and Mom was in hers. The house was so quiet except for the steamy, bubbling sounds from the stovetop.

I looked at my assignment sheet. Math was done. The only thing left was the poem. Mrs. Juarez asked us to write a poem about our favorite food. She was all excited about this nutrition unit and was trying to get us to be as excited. For kids who liked to write poems, like me, this would be fun. For kids who just liked to think about their favorite food, they could probably have fun doing this assignment, too.

My favorite food... Well, chocolate always pops right into my head when I think about food, but this was different. What *was* my favorite food? I guess I had never thought about it before. Sometimes I played a little game with myself where I would think, *What if you could only pick one book to read over and over again for the rest of your life? What book would I pick?* Maybe this sounds dumb, but I did it with lots of things, like TV shows, or songs. Sometimes at Haley's we would play this game, but we never applied it to food before, and now it seemed so obvious.

Well, I love bacon and eggs – a lot - but if I could only pick one food to eat for the rest of my life, would it be bacon and eggs? And maybe that counted as two foods. Cranberry nut bread, the kind I bake from the recipe on the back of the cranberry bag. I thought a long time about this one, and even wrote down some words that rhyme with cranberry. *Airy, dairy, fairy, ferry, hairy, Jerry, Mary, nary, Perry, query, scary, Terry, very, wary.*

Those were the easy words. I had a trick to find rhyming words – start at the beginning of the alphabet, and put each letter as the beginning sound. It works like a charm, except most of the words tend to be pretty short and it's easy to overlook words like *tributary.* Not that any of these words inspired anything, and besides, I wasn't one hundred percent convinced that I would want to eat cranberry nut bread for the rest of my life, either.

As I sat there thinking about the other foods I like, I realized for the second time that day that I was hungrier than I should be. Now my growling stomach was accompanying the pops and bubbles of the spaghetti sauce. I felt sick again. Not from hunger, but dread. Where was Dad? Would this be another one of those nights? It was hard to think about a favorite food poem when your dad might, at this very moment, be getting drunk somewhere. The sudden ringing of the phone broke the silence and my reverie. I grabbed the receiver. "Masons!"

"Rache, honey, put Mommy on." It was Dad, and he was sober!

Chapter 7 – Favorite Foods

I couldn't wait for school the next morning. It was one of those great fall mornings in Florida, cool after an extended summer, and even the wait for the bus felt good. At school, everyone was showing Mrs. Juarez the labels they brought in. There was everything from boring green beans (I'm glad I skipped that!) to a little box of Ben and Jerry's Chunky Monkey ice cream. It was fun.

We had two bulletin boards in our classroom, and Mrs. Juarez was always changing them to go along with the topic we were studying. The best part was, she always had figured out a way for us to have our work up there on display. Today one of the bulletin boards had been prepared for something new. She had stapled a red and white checkered plastic tablecloth to the bulletin board for the background, and now we were all wondering what would follow, although there was no doubt it would be related to nutrition.

"What's with the tablecloth, Miss Juarez?" That was Danny Fitzgerald. He always said "Miss So and So" whether the teacher was Miss, Mrs. or Ms. The only time he got it right was when we had a man teacher. I don't know why that bugged me, but it always did.

"You'll see," replied Mrs. Juarez. "The class is going to work on it today." I had a feeling it had something to do with our favorite food poems we had written the night before, but you never knew with Mrs. Juarez. When she was excited about a topic — which was always — you never knew what she'd come up with.

The morning flew by, and soon it was DEAR time. I brought an extra lemon poppy seed muffin to give to Alice Lee, but she declined. "No thanks," she whispered, "My mom packed my favorite!" Her eyes were big and she smiled as she held up an Oreo. I settled back to enjoy *two* lemon poppy seed muffins, and the latest developments with the murder in the graveyard. Not a real murder, but a scene from the book, *Tom Sawyer.*

I didn't know anything about the author, Mark Twain, but he sure had written a great book full of fascinating characters. I was just getting to the part where Injun Joe falsely accused Muff Potter of Doc Robinson's murder when Mrs. Juarez called out that DEAR time was over. Darn! Now the suspense would haunt me until I could resume my reading. I always had the feeling that even Mrs. Juarez was a little sorry to see DEAR time end so quickly.

After we got back to our desks (we could sit anywhere we wanted during DEAR time) Mrs. Juarez slid the Author's Chair from its corner. The Author's Chair was one of the best things about Mrs. Juarez's class. None of my other teachers had an Author's Chair. Oh, sure, you got to stand in front of the class and read something you wrote, but it was completely different in Mrs. Juarez's class.

She had this big, tall wooden stool with a back on it, and someone had painted "Author's Chair" across the back. Mrs. Juarez told us that *only* an author could sit in the chair to read something original. When she read us a story, even *she* couldn't sit there, even though it sat up high. One time our principal, Mr. Joseph, came in to read something to the class. He started to sit in the Author's Chair, and Mrs. Juarez jumped up and exclaimed, "Oh, Mr. Joseph, I'm so sorry but that's the *Author's* Chair, and only an author reading his or her original work can sit there to read!" She looked embarrassed, and so did he. Nobody laughed, which was a good thing.

So, here was Mrs. Juarez seating herself on the Author's Chair, and we all knew she had written something to read to us. "Last night you all wrote a poem about your favorite food, and you all know I never give you a creative writing assignment without trying it out myself."

This was true. When we made a class book, Mrs. Juarez always had a page to contribute. "So, I'm going to share my favorite food poem, and then I'd like to hear *your* poems." My classmates and I settled back to enjoy ourselves. Mrs. Juarez leaned her head back, smiled, and began to read:

The Sandwich
My brother made a sandwich of jelly, eggs, and goo,
Olives, ketchup, lettuce leaves, good old Elmer's Glue,

He topped it off with pumpernickel, bottomed it with rye,
And when he took a bite of it I thought that I would die!
He quickly took another bite, then swallowed – gulped it down,
A burp said he enjoyed it; I shuddered at the sound,
He used his sleeve to wipe his face and something on his chin,
The way he eats I just don't know how he can stay so thin.
He finished up, licked off his thumb and said he'd make another,
No one I know can eat more food than my skinny little brother!
He offered me a taste and said I really ought to try it,
"No way!" I said, "It's yucky, and besides, I'm on a diet!"
He shrugged and took another bite, he said it tasted good,
I thought perhaps I'd have a taste, I should – in fact, I would!
He held it out, I held my nose, I even shut my eyes,
(I hoped the paramedics way downtown could hear my cries!)
I nibbled on the crust, took a bite, began to chew…
Good grief! It was delicious! So I made myself one, too!

She smiled expectantly as she finished, and everyone clapped and cheered. "Oh, that was so cool, Mrs. Juarez!"

"Yeah, mine isn't that good. That was *great!*"

"Wow, Mrs. Juarez, that's your best poem yet!"

"Is that *really* your favorite food?"

"Elmer's Glue, my favorite!" Everyone was talking and making comments and getting out their poems in eager anticipation. I had mine all ready.

It had been easy. When my dad called last night and talked to my mom, I knew everything would be okay, so that made it easy to concentrate on my poem. Mom was talking to Dad while she set the table and, by the time she dumped the freshly boiled spaghetti into the colander he was walking through the door. Everyone was talking during supper except for me. I was thinking about my poem.

"...So that's why I like ice cream best, and hope this question's on our test!" Everyone laughed out loud. Darn, I'd been in La La Land for just a minute, thinking about last night, and I missed hearing Chris's poem. He was undoubtedly the funniest boy in our class, so I would have to ask him to let me read it later on. Everyone was smiling and some kids were still snickering about his poem as

Mrs. Juarez asked for the next volunteer. Hands went up, and the poetry reading continued.

I paid closer attention, afraid of missing something good. Some were short, and some went on and on. Libby read hers, something cute like, "Chinese, please..." and sailing the seven seas, and someone whispered loudly that she copied it from a Shel Silverstein book, but someone else said, "Shut up, you're just jealous." And so it went with Mrs. Juarez intervening here and there, praising and giving encouragement, and finally it was my turn.

I always get a little panicky at the last minute. What if it really isn't any good? What if I just *thought* it was good? But I smiled at Alice Lee and Haley and began to feel confident. Then I sat down in the Author's Chair, slid up to the edge of the seat so I could hook my feet on the rung, and began to read:

Surviving on Salsa

Stranded on a desert island, for what food do I wish?
Uncle Erik's special salsa in a great big dish,
He dices onions and tomatoes, adds peppers so it's hotter,
So when I scoop a chip full, my eyes begin to water.
For football games and hockey too, he'll bring a giant batch,

And two big bags of tortilla chips – now that's a perfect match,
I love the crunch, the spice, the zing - I cannot get enough,
Of Uncle Erik's salsa, and I eat until I'm stuffed.
I don't like Chili's, Rio Bravo's or that salsa in a jar,
I only like my uncle's – he's the Salsa Making Star.
It's Uncle Erik's recipe, he won't divulge the secret,
But luckily he makes a lot and always lets me eat it.
From Titusville to Timbuktu, from Toledo clear to Tulsa,
No one can match the supreme taste of Uncle Erik's salsa.

Whew! I looked up and smiled, climbed out of the Author's Chair and hurried to my seat. "Oh, Rache, that was so good. Wait'll your Uncle Erik hears it!"

"Yeah, Rachel, that was *so* good, you're making me hungry!" It was hard to hear their comments as my mind was going back over everything. Did I pronounce everything right? Did I read all the lines? I almost messed up the rhythm when I read the part with the cities. Everyone knew where Titusville was. Should I have left out all that stuff about Timbuktu and Tulsa? Well, the only other word I could think of that rhymed with salsa was balsa, that kind of wood Josh used to make model airplanes.

"*Very* nice, Rachel," Mrs. Juarez was saying. "Your uncle must make super salsa if you like it even better than Chili's! Are you *sure* he won't share that recipe?"

"No," I answered, "I've asked him a thousand times." It felt good to sit down and let someone else have a turn. My mind was racing, the way it always did at times like this. A combination of relief and exhilaration flooded through me. I loved school! And I was so lucky to be good at it. I always felt bad for kids who struggled and couldn't seem to grasp the material. I never minded waiting while the teacher went over it again and again. I just went to La La Land. In fact, I was already there.

Chapter 8 – Creative Homework Assignment

The bus ride home that day wasn't bad. Haley was planning one of her 'fabulous famous sleepovers', as she calls them, so there was a lot of talk about that, and I was still feeling great from how much everyone liked my poem. If I thought about my parents, I just tried to think about how nice everything was last night and push any other thoughts out of my head.

Haley was a riot. She related the instructions she had given her mother. "So, I just told my mom, you CAN'T come to the sleepover!"

"What'd she say?" asked Rebecca.

"Hmmph! Are you kidding?" Haley rolled her eyes and crossed her arms. For a minute she looked just like her mom, which made it even funnier. "She said, 'I have a news flash for you – I LIVE here!' Like I didn't know *that!* And I'm like, 'Mom, I KNOW you LIVE here, I just don't want you hanging out in the family room with us just because you want to watch *Disney* movies!'"

Rebecca giggled. "Who will make the food if she doesn't come?"

"What's there to make? We nuke some pizza rolls. The rest is just ice cream and junk anyway." She had a point. Mrs. Bennington really just hovered about on the pretense of preparing the snacks, but her real mission was to make sure no one missed what she called "the best parts."

"Girls, girls, now watch this part," she'd say, "this is where the girls discover they are really *twins* separated when they were babies!" Well, we had seen these videos a dozen times at least, so although we weren't quite the experts that Mrs. Bennington was, we were pretty sure we knew what was going on. Don't get me wrong, Mrs. B is so nice, and I love going over to their house. She was just kind of fanatical about her old movies. I didn't mind her hanging around during sleepovers, but apparently this was Haley's newest rebellion.

The bus lurched to a stop, and Rebecca and Haley continued the conversation as they waved goodbye. My mind wandered to the subject of homework. I had been right about the new bulletin board having something to do with our food poems. After we had all read our poems today, Mrs. Juarez showed us what she had in mind. A big stack of white paper plates sat by the homework basket. She held up one that was on her desk. You could see that she had drawn a picture of a sandwich on it, sort of like a cartoon, but more as a background. Then she had written her poem right over the picture. It was a nice effect, and she wanted us to take a paper plate home, illustrate our favorite food, and then write our poem across the picture. She planned to put all the paper plates on the tablecloth bulletin board, and it should look something like a picnic in progress.

Although I didn't regret writing about Uncle Erik's salsa, I was a little worried about how to actually *draw* salsa. It wasn't exactly an object, like Mrs. Juarez's sandwich. Uncle Erik, by the way, is my dad's older brother. He was responsible for getting my dad started in construction back before my parents got married. Uncle Erik built houses, and my dad helped. Dad always said that Uncle Erik taught him everything he knew about construction. Uncle Erik was a pilot now. Dad said Uncle Erik was always crazy about airplanes, even when they were kids, and one day he left work early for a flying lesson. After that, he flew every chance he got and eventually started his own charter business, which he's had for years now. Mom said Uncle Erik just handed the construction business over to my dad, who by then knew a thing or two about it, and they've both been in their element ever since.

Josh, Jeremy, and I adored Uncle Erik, our single favorite relative. He never stopped smiling, at least that's how it seemed, and he took us flying, too. Uncle Erik doesn't drink either, and sometimes I wondered how two brothers could be so different about something like that. Many times I thought about talking to Uncle Erik about my dad's drinking problem, but I could never get up the nerve. Besides, what exactly could I expect Uncle Erik to do?

"Mom, how do you draw salsa?" My mom was reading my poem and smiling.

"This is really good, honey. You'll have to read it to Uncle Erik next time you see him."

"Yeah, I will. But in the meantime, I have to do this paper plate." Josh came in to see what was going on.

"What's that for?" he asked. I explained my homework assignment, and he said he wished he had had Mrs. Juarez in fifth grade. "I had Mrs. Mercer, and everyone called her Mrs. Misery behind her back."

"They still do," I told him.

Maybe I could draw a big, colorful bowl with salsa sticking out at the top. No, Mrs. Juarez really wanted all the plates to look like they had food on them. I could just sort of scribble red to look like tomatoes with some green marks for the onions and peppers. I just had a funny feeling that wouldn't look right. I went in my room and poked around in my closet where I keep school supplies. I found my markers and then spotted a pack of construction paper. There was a bunch of brown and beige, colors I never had any use for, and then another color jumped out at me. I swear it was the color of tortilla chips!

I spread everything out on the kitchen table and got to work. I cut out a bunch of triangles to look like chips and laid them all around the edges of the plate, overlapping each other to look as much like chips as possible. Wow! It looked pretty good. I had tons of paper, so I took a couple paper chips and drew little black dots on them, the kind you see on corn chips. At first they were kind of big and looked kind of gross, so I tried a fine tip marker, and it was perfect! Great. I had a bunch of chips for around the edge of the plate. Now, how about the salsa?

I could write the poem in the center and then draw some little blotches of salsa around the words, but that didn't seem like it would work. Well, no matter what I did for salsa, I would have to write the poem on the plate. I used pencil so I could erase if I messed up and very carefully printed the words. Surviving on salsa... Forty-five minutes later my poem was neatly printed in the center of the plate, and the chips made a perfect frame. Okay, but what about the *salsa?* That was, after all, the subject of the poem. I had too many words. It took up the whole plate, and there was just no room to draw salsa.

Maybe I could take out a few lines. Mrs. Juarez might not even notice. But which lines? And I hated to start erasing and rearranging the poem. All of a sudden it hit me!

I grabbed a red fine tip marker and two shades of green and started tracing my letters in salsa colors. Most of the letters were red, but every few letters I'd trace in one of the greens. At first it looked all wrong, but it was too late to turn back now. Mrs. Juarez had only given us one paper plate, so I had to see it through. As I finished the lettering on the last word, *salsa*, I knew it was going to be fine. I carefully glued the paper chips around the edge, and in a few minutes I was done. Up close, there was a very legible poem. But when you stood back a few feet, the colored words just blended together and looked like a bowlful of Uncle Erik's salsa surrounded by chips. Whew! Mission accomplished.

C

hapter 9 – The Big Sleepover

"Okay, everyone, listen up!" Haley was barking orders. It was Friday night, and six of us had converged on her family room for the big sleepover. Alice Lee, Rebecca Shelton, Darla Whitley, Angie Dennis, Janelle Martin, and Michelle Luther-Smith. Michelle's mom used her maiden name and Michelle's dad's last name for Michelle's hyphenated last name. I think that's so neat, but I guess it never occurred to my parents. Then I would be Rachel Cooper-Mason.

"I SAID *listen up!*" Haley was standing on the ottoman as though it were a stage. Everyone quit talking and snapped to attention. Haley laid out the itinerary.

"Alright, as soon as my parents leave we'll get the food ready. I rented some *new* movies – don't worry, *I* picked them out! We'll bring both cordless phones in here, and we'll be all set."

She didn't really need to tell us what to expect. We had been having sleepovers at Haley's since first grade, and the routine never varied. The only thing different about tonight was the absence of Mr. and Mrs. Bennington. Or should I say, the absence of *Mrs.* Bennington. Mr. Bennington always said hi and then just disappeared, but Mrs. B was almost a fixture at the sleepovers. But Haley had convinced her that we didn't need her close supervision (or interference, as Haley saw it), so her mom had agreed to "give us our space," as Haley told us. Her parents weren't actually *leaving*, they were just going next door to visit the neighbors. They would be close by if we needed them.

I loved these sleepovers, and I was lucky to be part of such a great group of girls. Alice Lee, the one who shared her cookies with me at DEAR time, is probably the quietest of them, but when she starts to giggle, look out! She is kind of petite for her age and always looks like somebody's little sister, but she's actually the oldest of our group. Alice Lee has very fine blonde hair that she almost always wears in a ponytail except for special dress-up occasions.

Rebecca Shelton is something of a tomboy. She has short brown hair and bright rosy cheeks.

One time in second grade Danny Coleman teased her. "You're wearing your mom's make-up! Where's your lipstick?" Rebecca jumped on him and knocked him over and hit him with her fists. Danny started crying and tried to run away. It was on the playground, and our principal, Mr. Joseph, was out there talking to the custodian. He ran over and separated them, and even though Rebecca got in a lot of trouble, no one has ever made fun of her rosy cheeks since then.

Haley's cousin, Darla Whitley, didn't go to our school, but she was also in the fifth grade and had been at almost all of Haley's sleepovers down through the years. I didn't know her as well, but she's a lot like Haley. Darla and Haley both are great dressers. They always have the nicest outfits, and they're always going to the mall with their moms. Mrs. B and Darla's mom are sisters, so that probably explains their similarities.

Angie Dennis is probably my best friend. It's just that I ride the same bus with Haley and Rebecca, so I don't see Angie as much. Also, she's in Mrs. Mercer's class, and we're all in Mrs. Juarez's. Angie and I were really upset when we found out we wouldn't have the same teacher this year. We had been in the same class every year since second grade. Her mom tried to get Mr. Joseph to switch her, but he wouldn't do it. Angie is so much fun! She has the best sense of humor of anyone I know. I guess you could call her the class clown. She has long, thick hair, kind of blondish-brown, and dark brown eyes. She always gets picked to be in school plays and wants to be an actress when she grows up. As much as I like Haley's sleepovers, I would much rather go to Angie's house to spend the night.

Janelle Martin and Michelle Luther-Smith are best friends, and that makes sense since they're both boy crazy. They are *always* talking about boys, whether it's boys in our school or famous boy movie stars. That's why Haley brings both cordless phones into the family room during sleepovers. Janelle and Michelle will spend the whole evening calling boys and giggling into the receiver together. I don't know if the boys appreciate these phone calls or not, but Janelle and Michelle will always sit over in the corner away from the TV so they can carry on these long conversations. They each have a phone and talk to the same boy, obviously, and every now and then they'll both shriek and laugh, then everyone else turns around and says, "Shhhhhhhhhh...!"

Haley is the most confident girl I know. No wonder, since everything in her life is so perfect. She is the only child, so her mom buys her anything she wants. For instance, she has her own computer, her own TV and VCR in her bedroom, and her mom was already talking about what kind of car they would buy her when she turns sixteen! She takes every kid of lesson – ballet, tap, piano, gymnastics – and her mom is always signing her up for something new. Haley has gorgeous black hair, very shiny and long, and she wears it in so many styles you would think she was a model or something. I'm not exactly jealous of Haley, but I wouldn't mind a bit if my life were a little more like hers.

I've already described a lot about myself. As far as what I look like, well, I am really an okay looking person. Straight, brown hair, shoulder length, bangs. Blue eyes. Some freckles, but not too many. The only one in our group without pierced ears (I'm kind of afraid!). Besides being good in school and being a pretty good cook I'm a decent pitcher when we play softball. I also try to be a good friend.

The sleepover was going great. Janelle and Michelle were on the phones. Occasionally they would call out to us, "Jason (or some other boy) says hi!" We were used to this. Haley had plates of food set out, and she was going through the stack of movies she had rented. Scary movies, comedies, romances – all new releases. None of them were very good, which was just as well since Angie and I were using this time to catch up on things.

"You won't believe what Mrs. Mercer did today," she told me. "Right after she gave us our zillionth handout for the day, she sat down at her desk to work on her crossword puzzle. She does this *every* day, right after lunch. Well, we were all just ready to puke...*Circle the simple subject, underline the simple predicate*...doesn't she know we did this in fourth grade? Anyway, Drew Pickett started making faces at anyone who would look at him. You know how he is. So, he makes this hilarious face with his tongue hanging out. You should see how long his tongue is! So, I couldn't help myself. I made a gross face back at him." She reached up and stretched the skin below her eyes down and used her other hand to push her nose up – like a pig. I laughed out loud.

"Shhhhhhhh!" All the TV watchers hushed us.

"Yeah, that's just what Drew did. Only he snorted when he laughed, and Mrs. Mercer looked up just then and caught *me* making the face. She never said a word to Drew, who started the whole thing. "She goes, 'Angie Dennis, I am *sick* and *tired* of your antics! Go *straight* to see Mr. Joseph – NOW!' I couldn't believe it! She completely spazzed on me and sent me for a referral! Just for making faces!"

"Yeah, Josh said she was a real witch when he had her. I can't believe you got a referral, though."

"Well, Mr. Joseph was pretty nice about it, but he's giving me the old, 'This is a part of your permanent record' lecture, like I was some kind of convict or something. Actually, Mrs. *Misery* sends a couple kids for referrals every week. She is *such* a *witch*!"

"What did your mom say?"

Angie smiled. "She said, 'Next time you make faces make sure you're *not* facing Mrs. Mercer!'" Angie's mom is great like that.

Eventually all the girls had their sleeping bags unrolled and were curled up on pillows. Empty paper plates and soda cans were strewn about the room. Alice Lee was always the first one to fall asleep. She could sleep through the loudest screams of a horror movie. Michelle and Janelle had to hang up for good. The last boy they called yelled at them for calling so late. They looked like they would fall asleep any minute. Angie and I were always the last ones talking, but when everyone else had gone to sleep we finally said good night. The Benningtons' house was quiet except for the deep breathing of the sleeping girls. Mr. and Mrs. B had poked their heads in an hour or so earlier to say good night.

I settled into my sleeping bag and curled up on my side. This was the only part of the sleepovers I didn't like – trying to fall asleep. It took me hours, and then I was always the last one up in the morning. I couldn't help it – my imagination always kept me awake. Oh, it wasn't all the horror movies Haley had rented. I didn't even watch them. It's just that when I was away from home I never knew what might be going on. What if my dad had been drinking tonight? It was Friday night, the end of the week. What if at this very minute he was fighting with my mom? At home I fell asleep listening – listening for sounds of fighting, trying to hear if my mom called out. I couldn't listen here at Haley's.

I could've called home earlier, and I would've been able to tell what was going on. But, I didn't want the girls thinking I was a baby for calling home, and mainly, I didn't want them to think that there might be something wrong at my house. None of my friends knew about my dad, not even Angie. No one would understand. My dad is really great, and I didn't want anyone to think he was a bad person just because of this one thing he did. I could never tell anyone.

Chapter 10 – The Next Morning

Sure enough, I was the last person awake the next morning. I could hear everyone stirring around, but I was so tired from lying there half the night wondering about my mom and dad. Mrs. B came in to announce breakfast was ready.

"So, did you girls have a big night? What movies did you watch?" I could tell she felt excluded, but she always gave Haley her own way. "Come on, now, I have a nice big breakfast buffet all set up." She always did, too.

"Oh, French toast!" Janelle was filling up her plate. It all looked good; I didn't know what I wanted.

"Can I just have some cereal, please?" Alice Lee never ate anything but cereal for breakfast.

"Of course, Alice Lee. I think I remembered that your favorite is Cinnamon Toast Crunch." That was Mrs. Bennington. She was always making sure everything was just perfect for everyone.

"Mom, why'd you make hash browns?"

"What's wrong with hash browns, Haley? You eat them all the time."

Haley was just giving her mom a hard time. She started telling her about the nutrition lesson Mrs. Juarez had us do yesterday.

"Mom, are these those frozen hash browns, or did you cut up the raw potatoes yourself?" They were the frozen kind, and Haley surely knew this, but she ranted on about the nutritional value of certain foods. Alice Lee rolled her eyes at me. I'm sure we were thinking the same thing – Haley didn't care anything about nutritional values last night when she was scarfing down pizza rolls and pouring hot fudge onto her ice cream.

"Mrs. Juarez had us analyze the nutritional value of potatoes yesterday and the price per pound of these potato products. We checked out regular raw potatoes, a box of instant potatoes, a box of frozen hash browns, and a bag of chips. She had the receipt from the store, and get this – the more the potato is processed, like *frozen hash browns*, for instance – the less nutritional value it has, *and* the more expensive it is!" Haley was acting like her mom was trying to poison us while driving her family into bankruptcy.

Alice Lee, who was usually so quiet, asked, "So, Haley, is that why you ate half a bag of chips last night?" Haley gave her a dirty look, but Mrs. B looked relieved.

"Well, honey, I'll just have to get you to help me do the grocery shopping since you're learning so much about nutrition. Did you girls have fun writing your favorite food poem?" We explained to Darla and Angie about our assignment, and Angie complained that they never did anything fun or creative in Mrs. Mercer's class. "Haley wrote about ice cream," Mrs. B. smiled.

"Yeah," said Rebecca, "and guess what Mrs. Juarez is going to have us do on our test at the end of the unit? Based on all the things we learn about good nutrition, we all have to analyze our *own* favorite food and justify whether or not it's 'nutritionally sound' as she calls it. Too bad half the class picked ice cream as their favorite food!"

It was true. On the bulletin board, which looked great with all the paper plate poems and little plastic forks and spoons Mrs. Juarez hot-glued on the tablecloth, the words, "Favorite Foods: Nutritious or Not?" loomed large. We were all wondering how we would actually know how to analyze the food, but most of the kids had picked junk food anyway. Ever since we found out we had to analyze it I was a little worried. Remember, Uncle Erik's recipe was a big secret. If I didn't know what was in it, how would I know if it was nutritionally sound or not?

After breakfast we packed up our stuff and loaded into Mrs. B's minivan. As she dropped each girl off, she thanked us for coming. She was always so nice. Of course, everyone thanked her and told her what a great time we had. Girls were yelling, "Bye! See you Monday! See you next time!" I was thinking about home and hoping everything was all right.

Pretty soon we pulled into my driveway. My dad was in the yard with the weed whacker. He shut it off and said hi to Mrs. B. "Hey, Gloria, I hope Rachel behaved herself!" Dad smiled.

"Oh, Mike, she just *trashed* the place!" Mrs. Bennington laughed. It was just a joke, because I kind of had a reputation with the parents as being polite and well behaved.

"Bye, Haley, bye Mrs. B!" I slammed the door of the van. "See you Monday."

"Bye, Mike. Say hi to Tina. We'll have to get together one of these days!"

"Sure thing. Tell Jack we said hello."

It felt great to be home. I could tell by dad's attitude nothing had gone wrong last night. Just as Mrs. B was backing out my mom opened the door. She was waving and smiling. "Hi, Gloria! Thanks for having Rachel over!"

It was good to be home.

Chapter 11 – The New Boy

On Monday morning there was an air of excitement in the classroom. A new boy had joined our class. In Florida, new kids were nothing new – if that makes sense, but it always seemed like an event each time it happened. Every year a couple new kids came and a couple kids moved. I heard a teacher once describe it as the "transient nature of the Sunshine State".

His name was Adam Gopnik, and by DEAR time he seemed to have made the rounds of the entire class. For being new, he certainly wasn't shy. It was as though making new friends was something he did every day. He wasn't confident the way Haley was, with her perfect clothes and perfect life, but he was just confident. I got the impression that Adam Gopnik never worried whether people liked him or not.

"Isn't that a great book?" Adam whispered to me during DEAR time. "Did you get to the part yet where Tom and Becky wander off in the cave?"

I nodded. "This is the second time I've read it," I whispered, and then I put my finger to my lips. Mrs. Juarez didn't really say much if we whispered about the books we were reading, but I knew it was a rule to be quiet during DEAR time, and I'm not much of a rule breaker.

"Have you read *Huckleberry Finn*?" Adam asked. I shook my head and put my head down to read my book. I didn't want to get in trouble. *Huckleberry Finn.* I knew about the character because of reading *Tom Sawyer,* and I had flipped through it once in the library. It was written in the voice of Huck Finn, and I knew someday I would have to read it. Haley had the video, but she never wanted to watch it.

At lunch, Adam was the center of attention. He knew something about everything, but he wasn't a know-it-all. He was from Jacksonville, so Florida wasn't new to him. He liked to surf, had been to California, and said his favorite subjects were science and reading. His hair was light brown with blond streaks, probably from the sun. He was very tan and looked strong for a fifth grade boy. When he smiled, his whole face smiled, kind of like Uncle Erik's. He told us he had two older brothers – half-brothers – who were in their twenties! He said his dad had been married before. Adam seemed so different from everyone, and yet he fit right in. I tried to imagine how I would be if I had to move to a new school in the middle of fifth grade. I would hate it.

But Adam not only didn't hate it, he seemed to like it. Before lunch was over he had made plans to meet Mark Langdon after school to go surfing. "You'll love our beach," Mark told him. "We get some pretty good waves." I knew Mark surfed a little, but I didn't know if he was any good at it. He probably is, though, because he was good at other sports.

We were all talking and laughing when we walked into our classroom after lunch. Book orders! The book orders were there! Once a month or so, Mrs. Juarez passed out book orders. I *loved* the book orders! We were given a little flyer that listed all kinds of books, and they weren't very expensive. We could turn in our money and order them, and in a few weeks, when we least expected it, we'd come in from lunch and our new books would be on our desks. Not everyone bought books, but my mom always let me get some. Josh and Jeremy also bought books, so all three of us had a nice stash of books in our rooms at home. I loved the smooth feel of the new covers and the smell of ink as I flipped through the pages. *The Adventures of Tom Sawyer* – now I had my own copy! It looked different from Mrs. Juarez's copy, with different illustrations. I also got *Esio Trot* by Roald Dahl, a book of poems, and *A Single Shard* by Linda Sue Park.

My mom used to get book orders when she was a kid, which is why she lets us buy them, I guess. She still had all her books from when she was a kid, and when I was younger she used to read them to us. My favorite was *The Secret Language* by Ursula Nordstrom. It was about two girls at boarding school. Boarding school sounded kind of glamorous to me, but sad at the same time. I knew I would get homesick, or be worrying all the time about whether or not my parents were fighting. Or, maybe at boarding school I could just forget all my worries and have adventures like Martha Sherman and Victoria

North, the two main characters in the book. Once they had a midnight feast and got caught, and once they built a little clubhouse in the woods. They had a secret language, just a couple words, really, that no one else knew. When I was little and my mom read it to me, she skipped the chapter where Victoria found out there isn't really a tooth fairy. I was kind of young, and my mom didn't want to spoil it for me. I found out she skipped it when I read the book myself a couple years later.

"Looks like some good reading, Rache." Haley was checking out my books. She always bought books, too, usually *Harry Potter* books. Mrs. Juarez always bought books from the book orders, too. She kept adding to our class library, and she would buy all kinds of books – science fiction, historical novels, you name it. I noticed Alice Lee looking at the new stack on Mrs. Juarez's desk. She had just picked up *The Giver* by Lois Lowry and was thumbing through it when the fire alarm rang. It startled her so badly she ripped half the cover off the book! Alice Lee looked horrified. She looked around quickly to see if anyone had noticed. The other students were quietly streaming through the door as Mrs. Juarez said, "That's it, nice and quietly, thank you…"

We headed single file for the playground, the routine of the fire drill. Everyone was quiet and well behaved. You never knew if it was the real thing or not. Once there was a fire in the cafeteria, but they put it out before the fire department arrived.

It turned out to be just a fire drill, and soon we were marching back to class. I remembered Alice Lee and the book and looked back at her. Her face was blanched, and she had a sick, scared look on her face. I felt so bad for her. Mrs. Juarez wouldn't yell at her or anything, but tearing the teacher's new book, even accidentally, was enough to ruin your day.

We all settled in quietly now and began the assignment Mrs. Juarez had on the board. It was a quick math warm-up before the lesson. When we finished, Mrs. Juarez was holding the torn book and looking around the classroom. Alice Lee looked like she would burst into tears at any minute.

"Before we go on, I was hoping we could clear up this matter." Mrs. Juarez held up the book and continued. "Apparently someone accidentally tore the cover of this new book. Accidents do happen, but it is important that we remember our class rule regarding honesty. I would appreciate if whoever tore this book would speak to me after class." That was just like Mrs. Juarez. She wouldn't embarrass you in front of the whole class. Alice Lee looked down at her desk. Her face was ashen and I felt just awful for her. She is so quiet and shy, and even though Mrs. Juarez wouldn't do anything to her – it was an accident, after all – Alice Lee looked scared to death.

Just as Mrs. Juarez laid the book down and was preparing to go over the math lesson, Adam Gopnik jumped up and blurted out, "I did it!" You could hear the collective intake of breath as the entire class gasped in disbelief. The new boy, Adam, the boy everyone liked, had accidentally torn the teacher's new book and was now *publicly* accepting responsibility! I couldn't believe it. After all, I knew Alice Lee had torn it when the fire alarm sounded. I looked at Alice Lee. Her mouth and eyes were wide open. No one was more stunned than she.

"I'm very sorry, Mrs. Juarez. I was about to tell you when we had the fire drill. I can pay you for the book." Adam looked sincerely remorseful. Alice Lee looked sincerely relieved.

"That won't be necessary, Adam, and I certainly appreciate your honesty. I will tape the cover and it will be fine."

Honesty. Well, *I* knew it was a lie, Alice Lee knew it was a lie, and Adam himself knew it was a lie. In fact, he probably had no idea *who* had torn the book! Oh! It was Tom Sawyer! No, no, it wasn't Tom Sawyer who tore the book, but it was a scene right out of *Tom Sawyer*. It was the scene where Becky Thatcher had accidentally torn the teacher's book, but Tom accepted the blame *and* the whipping that came with it! Oh my gosh! Adam Gopnik, the new boy, was just like Tom Sawyer!

Chapter 12 – Perfect Partners

By the winter break Adam Gopnik had become the most popular boy in our class. Not that anyone was jealous of his popularity. He was just genuinely nice. And he knew the most interesting things. He was a whiz in science and always had something unusual to add to the discussions. Mrs. Juarez was grateful for his enthusiasm, and it seemed to be contagious. When we went on a field trip to Cape Kennedy, Adam regaled us during the entire bus ride with distances to stars and planets, explained the concept of a black hole, and taught us all the words to *The Galaxy Song* by *Monty Python*. And Alice Lee, who never had a crush on a boy her entire life, was clearly smitten with Mr. Adam Gopnik. I never told anyone the truth about that day. There didn't seem to be any point in revealing what Adam wished to remain a secret. And no one understood secrets better than yours truly.

Adam was a whiz on computers, too. And his parents never minded if a houseful of kids showed up to visit. Adam was clearly an asset to our class. One day after school a bunch of us were hanging out, and he said, "Hey, I'll bet you didn't know I'm a famous writer!"

Nothing surprised us when it came to Adam, so we were ready for any explanation he offered. There on the coffee table was a stack of magazines, *The New Yorker*. "Look at this!" Adam flipped open one of the magazines and showed us an article by – no kidding – Adam Gopnik!

"Hey! Is that really *you*?"

"Wow, Adam, did you really write this? What's it about? What is this, anyway?"

Everyone was grabbing the magazine trying to read the article, and Adam started to laugh. "No, it's not really me," he confessed. "One time I was doing a search on the Internet for the name 'Gopnik' since it's so unusual, and here was this guy, Adam Gopnik who's a writer. I found out he writes a lot for *The New Yorker*, so my dad subscribed to it for me. It's mostly political, but I like it anyway. Once I wrote to him, and he actually wrote me back."

"No way! Are you related or anything?"

"Is he rich?"

"Did you ever meet him?" Everyone called out in amazement.

"No, we're not related, but he wrote me this letter wishing me luck in school and writing and all that. He said to 'keep in touch' so maybe I will."

We were amazed and *not* amazed at the same time. You had to know Adam to understand. He was just so different from everyone else.

Winter break lasted two weeks, and Mrs. Juarez had assigned research projects to be done over the break. "Some break!" Kenny complained, but when he found out the details of the assignment he was less critical.

"Research is something you do all the time," Mrs. Juarez had explained. "Every time you're curious about something and you try to find out about it, you're doing research. When we return from the winter break, we're going to get started on a unit about Florida – its history, culture, environment – all aspects of the Sunshine State. So, what I would like you to do is some head start research. You'll be working with a partner, so this will give you an opportunity to visit with one of your classmates during the break. I have listed several topics on these pieces of paper." She shook a little basket filled with folded white slips. "And, I have all your names in *this* basket." It was starting to sound fun to everyone.

"Rachel, would you pull the first name, please?" I reached into the basket and grabbed a slip.

"Haley Bennington!" I exclaimed. Great! My partner would be Haley – or so I thought.

"Thanks, Rachel. Haley, now will *you* pull a slip, and that will be your partner." Oh, rats! Mrs. Juarez had a different system going.

"Alice Lee Whittington!" Oh, great! Now I was starting to worry. Right from the start two of my best friends were taken. I wondered who I would get stuck with. Don't get me wrong – I like working with a partner, but sometimes, depending on my partner, I would get stuck doing all the work.

Mrs. Juarez continued bouncing around the room with her basket of names. Everyone was being partnered off, and my name hadn't been pulled yet.

Mrs. Juarez pulled the next name. "Adam Gopnik!" She handed the dwindling basket of names to Adam. He reached in and fished around.

"Rachel Mason!" He smiled at me and gave a thumbs-up. Well, working with Adam wouldn't be bad at all. As soon as we all had a partner, Mrs. Juarez started Phase Two of the assignments. Each team got to pull a slip, and that was to be our research topic. I knew Adam was hoping for something scientific, and I was hoping it would involve creative writing. *Henry Flagler, the beaches, the citrus industry, tourism...* Some of the topics sounded good, others didn't seem so interesting. Mrs. Juarez waved the basket at me. "Rachel, see what topic you and Adam will be researching." I clutched a slip and opened it with the anticipation I reserve for reading a Chinese fortune cookie.

"Manatees," I read aloud. I looked at Adam. He was beaming. Well, good. He probably already knew a lot about manatees, and even though I didn't see any creative writing possibilities I figured it would be fun working on a project with Adam Gopnik.

Mrs. Juarez passed out a list of possible projects. We were to learn *who, what, when, where, why, how* and *"so what"* about our topic and then compile the information into a project of some sort. The list was great! We could make a board game, do a computer presentation, write a song, make a video – there were at least 50 options! Mrs. Juarez really was the best teacher. I felt bad for Angie who was undoubtedly sitting at her desk across the hall filling out some boring worksheet.

So, that's how I came to be researching manatees with Adam Gopnik during our winter break. We started at his house doing research on the Internet. We found out there was a "Save the Manatees" club and everything. When we told his parents about our project, his dad said, "Oh, I've got just the song for you." His parents *loved* beach music and songs about the ocean. They had a big old-fashioned jukebox in their family room, and it was full of songs by the Beach Boys. Adam's dad had it rigged so you didn't have to put money in, and sometimes we'd just play music for hours.

"Listen to this," his dad was saying as he opened a CD case. He slid the CD into the player and skipped to the song. It was Jimmy Buffett, another singer whose songs were on their jukebox.

Sometimes I see me, as an old manatee, headin' south as the water's grow colder,

Tries to steer clear of the hum drum so near, it cuts prop scars deep in his shoulder...

It was a pretty song, not really about manatees, though, except for that one part.

"That's great, Dad. I forgot about that song. Maybe we can use that clip to go along with part of our presentation." Adam and I had agreed we would do a computer presentation and make a display to set up in the classroom. We were learning a lot about manatees and wanted to be experts when we gave our presentation to the class in January.

Chapter 13 – Christmas Shopping

Christmas was just two days away. Adam and I had completed a lot of our research, so we were giving the manatee project a rest until after Christmas. Mr. Gopnik had offered to take us to Blue Spring State Park after Christmas so we could see some live manatees, so we had that to look forward to in the not so distant future.

Our house was festive. Dad and Josh had hung lights on the outside, and Mom, Jeremy, and I decorated inside. We had a live tree, and even though the needles made a mess and I had to run the vacuum every day, it smelled like Christmas and I didn't mind a bit. Mom baked cookies and the boys and I decorated them. Things had been going smoothly. Mom and Dad hadn't had a bad fight in a while, so the only thing on my mind was Christmas!

Haley called that afternoon. "Hey, wanna come over and watch some Christmas videos?"

I hesitated. It was always fun at Haley's, but I was having fun at my own house. "I can't," I lied. "I have to help my mom with all this baking. Uncle Erik's coming to visit."

"Darn. There's nothing to do here." Haley was hinting that I should invite her over. Although I did invite her over once in a while, I always tried to avoid it. None of my friends had ever seen my parents fight, and any time I had someone over I would just dread something going wrong.

"Well, I would ask you to come over, but I think my dad wants me to go shopping with him later. - to help pick something out for my mom." This wasn't a hundred percent true. I knew my dad always put off shopping until the last minute, but he hadn't actually asked me to go along and help. Still, I was hoping he would.

"Well, call me when you get back and tell me what he got her." I hung up the phone and resumed my cookie decorating. A few minutes later Dad came whizzing into the kitchen.

"Mmmmm, don't look now, but the Cookie Monster has invaded the kitchen!" Dad stuffed a cookie into his mouth and gave me a hug. He smelled good – like fresh air, and his flannel shirt was soft. "So, if you're almost done with these cookies, maybe you'd ride along to the store with me and help me find a Christmas present for Mommy?"

He always called her 'Mommy' to us kids, even though we had stopped calling her mommy when we were little. "Really? Sure, I can go any time!"

Wow! It was as though he had heard my conversation with Haley. I loved doing stuff with my dad - especially when it was just the two of us.

"Tina," Dad called.

Mom came into the kitchen. "Rache and I are going shopping." He winked at me. "Is there anything you need while we're out?"

Mom grinned.

"Oh, just a gallon of milk, some laundry detergent, and maybe a string or two of pearls."

"Oh, is that all? Think we can remember that, Rache, honey?" Dad kissed mom on the cheek. "See you in a while…" and we were off.

It was exciting. Even though it was early in the evening, it was already getting dark. Most of the houses in our neighborhood were decorated, and the lights glowed brightly as we drove by. "Yep," Dad was saying, "I'd have to give first place to 125 Silver Palm Drive!" I laughed. That was *our* house. We got on the interstate and headed for the mall. It was sure to be packed, but Dad always said he liked the hustle and bustle of the stores right before Christmas, and besides, he had no idea how they were at any other time because he was such a procrastinator!

Jingle Bell Rock came on the radio and we sang along. It was going to be a great evening. The mall was crowded, so we had to park all the way out on the edge of the parking lot. Dad was in great spirits as we headed inside. In no time at all he was showing me sweaters and asking, "What do you think, Rache, is this Mommy?" Some were nice, and some were awful. We laughed a lot and made our way through the mall as my dad bought Christmas presents for my mom. *Why couldn't it always be this perfect*, I thought. Why couldn't Dad stop drinking forever and just be himself, the way he was right now? I hate to admit it, but I always thought he would. Every single time it happened I believed it would never happen again. I pushed those unhappy thoughts out of my head, though, and just concentrated on how much fun we were having.

Wow! What a haul! Mom was going to love her presents. Even though he waited until the last minute, Dad always found the best stuff for her. On the way out of the mall we saw Mr. and Mrs. Graves, our next-door neighbors. Two years ago a bad windstorm blew part of their giant live oak tree across our fence. It was a mess, and the fence was smashed to smithereens. Mr. Graves is really old, and he was so upset about it. My dad went over with his chainsaw and cleaned it up. Josh, Jeremy, and I helped pick up limbs and carried them out on a pile by the road. Mr. Graves kept thanking my dad over and over. "My word, Mike, anyone else would've slapped a lawsuit on me or something. And you don't say a thing, you just come out and clean it up. My word! We sure are grateful to have such good neighbors." That's how my dad is. He would do anything to help anybody. Now when we saw the Graves they called out, "Mike, Rachel... Merry Christmas!" Mr. Graves shook my dad's hand, and Mrs. Graves hugged me. They're very nice and don't have any family here. We talked a few minutes before saying good night. See? Everyone who knew my dad just loved him.

Chapter 14 – Christmas Surprises

It was Christmas morning! I always thought I'd be the first one up, but I could hear someone else stirring. I looked at my clock. Six-fifteen. I got up and made my way into the family room. I was still sleepy, but too excited to go back to bed. Mom was in the kitchen quietly baking cinnamon rolls. Gee, even if I hadn't heard her, the smell of cinnamon would've caught my attention.

"Merry Christmas, Rachel!" Mom whispered through a wide smile. "Give me a hug." She put her arms around me and hugged me and kissed the top of my head. Then she gave me the noogie patrol, but not hard. She always gave the noogie patrol when she was in a good mood. It was Christmas morning! The whole world was in a good mood!

"Want to help?" Mom asked.

"Sure." What I *really* wanted was to wake up Josh and Jeremy and jump into those presents under the tree, but it was fun having this quiet time with Mom.

"Mom, you're going to *love* what Dad got you," I whispered.

"Shhhh – no telling." She smiled and handed me two round pans. "Grease these, honey, while I put on the coffee." Mom made coffee while I got the pans ready. Then she got two more tubes of cinnamon rolls out of the fridge. No one ever wanted *real* breakfast on Christmas morning, just something to keep from starving to death while we opened our presents. In a few minutes the cinnamon rolls were baking and the aroma drifted further throughout the house. Ten minutes later the melting icing dripped down the edges, and three sleepy boys emerged from their beds.

"Merry Christmas!" Jeremy shouted. "Merry Christmas! Did Santa come?" None of us believed in Santa any more, but we pretended to on Christmas morning.

"Oh, Santa came, alright! One of the reindeer got a sandspur in its hoof, and Santa woke me up in the middle of the night to borrow the tweezers!" Dad smiled and winked at me. Mom and I carried plates and rolls, Dad grabbed two cups of coffee, and Josh and Jeremy brought a half-gallon of milk and three empty glasses into the family room. The tree lights were on. Mom must have turned them on when she got up. Presents were heaped under the tree, and the stockings bulged.

"Woo hoo!" yelled Josh. "The fat man *did* come!"

"Hey, who's calling me a fat man? And what's all the racket about? Can't a guy get any sleep around here?"

"*UNCLE ERIK!*" My brothers and I yelled in unison.

"Uncle Erik! When did you get here?" Everyone was talking at once. I rushed in to hug Uncle Erik. He rubbed my head with his big, strong hand and hugged the boys with his free arm. We were all just crazy about Uncle Erik. Oh, now it really *was* Christmas!

"Uncle Erik, I didn't mean *you* were the fat man," Josh laughed. "I didn't even know you were here! Mom said you weren't coming 'til dinnertime."

"Well, turns out I had a charter last night to Gainesville, and since I was so close I just came on in.

Called your dad about two this morning, and it turns out this is the wrong place to be for a guy who needs his sleep!"

"No kidding," yawned Dad, reaching for his coffee mug. Coffee! I hurried into the kitchen and got the "World's Greatest Pilot" mug from the cupboard. Josh had bought it for Uncle Erik two years ago, and Uncle Erik said he would keep it here so he knew he would always be guaranteed a good cup of coffee. I poured the hot brew into the mug and was proud to remember the ice cube. Plop! Uncle Erik *always* put one ice cube into his cup of coffee, and I always remembered, too. He was the only person I knew who did this, and it was just something else to love about him, although I don't really know why.

"Here's some coffee, Uncle Sleepyhead." He gratefully accepted the steaming mug and tweaked my cheek.

"Rache, honey, you're a thoughtful sweetheart, just like your mom!" Dad and Uncle Erik always call me "Rache honey." I like the way it sounds when they say it.

Suddenly Jeremy threw his hands up in the air. "It's Christmas, remember? Am I the only person who wants to see what the fat man brought?"

"Okay, okay," said Mom, "let's settle in for some unwrapping. Josh, will you please grab an empty trash bag for the paper?" Two seconds later Josh, the world's greatest procrastinator, magically produced the bag. Christmas morning had amazing effects on people. "Thank you, Josh. Okay, you all know the routine. Before you start tearing the paper off of everything, you have to pick out one present to save for later."

We already knew this and were already perusing the packages strewn under the tree. It was a family custom Mom had started. She always made us choose one gift to set aside until bedtime. That way, she had told us, the anticipation of Christmas lasted all day. It did, too. The hard part was always choosing the gift. When we were small, she did it for us. But when we got older we got to select it ourselves. Once I chose the tiniest package because of its size. Anything that small couldn't be anything great. I almost forgot about it by bedtime, then when

Mom reminded us we still had one present to open, I found myself wishing I had picked something better. Imagine my surprise when I unwrapped a beautiful golden ring with a bright green stone!

"That's emerald – your birthstone," Mom told me. She was grinning and trying not to laugh – at the look on my face, I suppose. She had guessed my strategy and had gone along smugly all day just knowing how shocked I'd be when I discovered this beautiful little ring. "See, the best things *do* come in little packages!"

After that, there was no logic involved when it came to selecting our Christmas night present. If we *could* discern which gift was best (which we *couldn't*), a part of us wanted to open it right then and there, and another part of us wanted to save it for last – delayed gratification, as Mom called it. So, here we were, dying to rip into our presents, but tortured by poking, shaking, and smelling them – hey, you had to be open-minded! – as we tried to make up our minds. Suddenly I came to a smallish package that didn't have Mom's handwriting on the name tag. *Uncle Erik!* That's it! I would save Uncle Erik's gift for last.

"I have mine!" I held it high above my head and smiled at Uncle Erik. He winked at me as he chewed on a cinnamon roll. Now the pressure was on Josh and Jeremy. Jeremy had been vacillating between his largest gift and his smallest gift. I knew the feeling... "Aw, heck," he said, and grabbed a completely different present. He just wanted to get on with the business of unwrapping, and he must have decided he couldn't wait to see what was inside those other two packages. Now it was down to Josh, the procrastinator.

"Come on, Josh," pleaded Jeremy. I knew better than to try to rush him. Josh masterfully resisted pressure of any form. Jeremy suddenly realized he was hungry and wisely decided to use this time to eat. I grabbed a cinnamon roll and poured a glass of milk.

"Don't you want an ice cube in that milk?" Uncle Erik teased me. When I was little, for a long time I would put an ice cube in my milk because of the way Uncle Erik drank his coffee. Even when Josh and Jeremy teased me I didn't care. But then I finally decided it was kind of silly. The milk was already cold, and the ice cube just watered down the milk.

"Okay, I have one," Josh reported. Mom put the three presents with the three she, Dad and Uncle Erik had picked. I was so busy looking through mine I didn't even notice them choosing theirs. Hey, Uncle Erik had picked *my* present to him!

For the next thirty minutes paper and ribbons flew through the air as we took turns opening, oohing, and ahhing. Christmas was undoubtedly the best day of the year! We passed around each other's gifts to a chorus of "Isn't that *nice?*" and "Thank you *so much!*" I got some new clothes including the new jacket I had been wanting. I put it on, zipped it up, and continued opening my loot. Rollerblades (with knee pads and elbow pads), and a little portable CD player for my bedroom! What a haul! There were other little things, like school supplies and a little blue diary with a key. Josh had bought me a package of 200 markers – all different colors, and Jeremy gave me a package of five notebooks with a different design on every cover and five matching pencils. I loved everything!

A little dazed by all the excitement, but absolutely undaunted, Jeremy yawned widely and looked up at the fireplace mantel. "Stockings!" he shouted.

"Bring 'em on!" echoed Josh.

Stockings! Wonderful, mysterious, bulging stockings! The toe, the toe – what was in the toe? Here was Santa's (Mom's!) masterpiece tradition. Every year we found sweet treats and tiny treasures in our stockings, but oh, the suspense of the toe! It was tradition that the most unique and splendid gift somehow fit in the toe of each stocking. No matter what it was, and it could be the most insignificant item to some people, it held special meaning for its recipient. It truly was the highlight of Christmas morning. No one was ever disappointed.

"Here you go!" Mom was passing out the stockings. I trembled inside. It wasn't as though you received a million dollar lottery ticket or anything, it's just that it was always so special!

We waited until every stocking was handed out. Mom even kept a stocking for Uncle Erik since he always came for Christmas. His name was neatly embroidered across the top, just like ours: *Dad, Mom, Joshua, Rachel, Jeremy, Uncle Erik.* We were all gently squishing our stockings and probing the shape of the toe. Mine felt a little empty in the toe area, but I wasn't concerned, only mystified. "Okay," said Mom, who could see the suspense was killing us, "let's see who got lumps of coal."

We began the careful unloading process. "Aw, thanks, Tina... cashews!" Uncle Erik loved cashew nuts, and Mom always put our favorite treats in the tops of our stockings. M&M Peanuts for Josh, Almond Joys for Dad, peanut butter cups for Josh, and Snickers for me. Mom wasn't left out. The rest of us conspired to fill her stocking, and she smiled as she pulled out a little box of petit fours.

We foraged on. Gel pens, bookmarks, Pez poppers. Fun gifts that fit inside a stocking. A piece of paper, rolled into a scroll. A gift certificate for CDs! For my new CD player! "Mom! Thank you!" I started thinking about all the CDs I wanted to buy as I reached deeper into my stocking, nearing the toe. A book. Which one? It was wedged tightly in the bottom of my stocking. I had to work to retrieve it.

This must be my toe gift. *The Adventures of Huckleberry Finn.* "Mom! *Huck Finn*! You knew I wanted this!"

"Yes, I know you keep re-reading *Tom Sawyer*, so I knew this would be special." It looked used, and Mom explained, "It's an old edition with special illustrations by the artist, Norman Rockwell." It was beautiful, and I flipped through looking at the pictures. Some of the characters were new, and some I recognized from *Tom Sawyer*.

"Thanks, Mom, I can't wait to read it!" It was a great toe gift, and I was feeling pretty good. My sagging stocking lay on the floor at my feet.

"I think you need to empty your stocking, Rachel," Mom's eyes twinkled. She obviously knew something I didn't know. I thrust my arm in up to my elbow. Sure enough, my fingers grasped another thin, paper-like item. I fished around to be sure there was nothing else, then carefully withdrew what felt like a card. I speculated. Another gift certificate. But for what? Where? I looked at it. It was wrapped in shiny gold paper and was a little crumpled from being jammed inside the toe. I unwrapped the paper trying not to further bend or crease whatever was inside. A hand-made sleeve covered a small card. "TOP SECRET!" was scrawled on both sides. "TO BE READ BY RACHEL MASON **ONLY!!!**" was printed underneath. Gee! Now *this* was a mystery!

"What is it? Let me see!" Jeremy, intrigued by the cryptic message, lunged toward the card.

"Jeremy! Settle down!" Mom scolded. I turned sideways and held the card so only I could see it. I carefully slid it from its sleeve. It could be a treasure map or something! (Well, it *could!*)

"OH MY GOSH! OH MY GOSH!" I repeated. On a three-by-five index card, neatly printed in his best handwriting was the secret recipe for "Uncle Erik's Salsa Recipe."

Chapter 15 – A Perfect Day

"Uncle Erik, I still can't believe you gave me your secret recipe!" He had just awakened from a nap on the couch and was evidently worn out by his late flight. Mom was in the kitchen. I could hear her chattering on the phone to someone as she prepared Christmas dinner. Dad was helping her, and the boys were in the family room playing a new computer game. I had Uncle Erik all to myself. "I didn't think you would ever tell anyone." I had already memorized it and hidden the recipe card in my bedroom. "What are 'Rotel' tomatoes?"

Uncle Erik yawned and grinned. "You'll find them at most grocery stores in the canned tomato section. I'm glad you weren't disappointed with your 'toe gift.' Your mom told me something about a little poem you wrote, and what was I supposed to do?" I blushed. I *did* want Uncle Erik to read my poem, but now I felt a little embarrassed, so I changed the subject a little.

"Yeah, well, the hard part was when we had the final exam on our nutrition unit. The last question was about the favorite food we had picked. We were supposed to analyze the ingredients, amounts, and serving size and determine if it was 'nutritious or not'. I told Mrs. Juarez the recipe really was secret, so she let me analyze the label from a jar of salsa she bought at the grocery store. Of course, it wasn't all that nutritious, and it wasn't even my favorite food."

"Well, I'm flattered, and now I've passed the secret on to you so you can have your favorite food any time you want it." I worried whether or not I could make it as well as Uncle Erik did. After all, I knew from experience that recipes didn't always turn out the way you thought they would. Kind of like life, I thought.

Mom and Dad came in and sat down. Mom looked tired. "Whew! I got up too early," she smiled. She looked kind of funny wearing jeans and a t-shirt and the pearl necklace and earrings Dad had bought her. "They're so beautiful," she had said when she opened them. She had put them on, then, and apparently forgotten to take them off. Mom could be a little absent-minded when she was distracted.

"Something sure smells good in the kitchen," Uncle Erik said. "Turkey and stuffing?"

"*And* pumpkin pie and pecan pie!" Dad chimed in.

"It'll be an hour or so 'til we eat," Mom said. "If you're going to go down to the new house, now might be a good time."

'The new house' was the latest house my dad was building. Whenever Uncle Erik came to visit, the two brothers always went to see Dad's latest project. "That sounds good," said Uncle Erik. "You wanna come along, Rache, honey?"

"Sure!" I had been planning to call Angie to see what she got for Christmas, but I could do that later. Dad and Uncle Erik talked the whole way there about construction in general – suppliers, subcontractors, building inspections – all topics of conversation I'd heard a million times. Finally we pulled in. There was no yard yet, just the graded area that would be landscaped after the house was finished, and the exterior was still just covered in Tyvek.

Walking inside the pungent smell of sawdust, drywall, and cool concrete filled my nostrils. I loved the smell of a new house. I had been to this one a couple times already and knew my way around. I wandered off to see what progress had been made while Dad showed Uncle Erik around.

In the family room, the stained glass window was not yet installed. That was always the first thing I looked for – the stained glass window, the trademark of my dad's houses. The opening was there for it, so I knew its shape, but it was covered over by a piece of plywood. It was always one of the last things to be done because Dad didn't want it getting broken accidentally by a worker's ladder or something. There was a wide window seat between two large bookshelves on one of the walls. It looked so cozy and inviting, even in the hollow emptiness of the unfinished room. I would like a window seat. When I grow up and get married, I want my dad to build my house. I want a window seat and a stained glass window.

"Whatcha think?" Dad and Uncle Erik joined me.

"Dad, can't you put a window seat in *our* house?" Dad laughed and looked at Uncle Erik.

"No detail escapes her keen eye. She would have me remodel that house on a monthly basis if she could." They continued their tour of the house. I came up behind them on the closed-in patio and overheard Dad tell Uncle Erik, "Yeah, if things don't improve soon I'm not sure what I'll do."

I stopped and tried to listen, but they had unlatched the screen door and their voices faded as they walked away. What things? What needed to improve? What was Dad worried about? My imagination always made me think the worst, no matter how hard I tried. Was business bad? Was it something about Mom? I don't know if other kids worry about their parents like I do, but I couldn't help myself. When they fought, I was afraid they would get a divorce. Sometimes, I almost wished they would. And since my dad was self-employed, I worried about his business. I knew that the construction business had its ups and downs, but we had always managed to do all right, at least it seemed that way to me. And maybe nothing was wrong at all. Sometimes people just said things like that to vent, or over something relatively minor. It was probably nothing at all. Despite my constant worrying, I remained a diligent optimist.

One good thing about having a vivid imagination is that I could push the worries out of my mind with new and improved replacement thoughts. Sort of an instant La La Land. So, I wandered on through the new house, imagining the kind of house I would live in when I grew up.

Later, after dinner, I cleared the table and Jeremy and Josh did the dishes. It was another Christmas tradition. Dad's idea, I think, to give Mom a break. The doorbell rang as Josh and Jeremy threw the dishtowel down and ran to continue their computer game. I picked up the towel, which had landed on the floor, and went to see who it was.

"Angie!"

"Can't stay! Here's your present!" She threw a package at me as her mom and dad waved from the car, the motor running.

"Wait! Here's yours!" I gave her my present. "Can't you open it now?" She looked over her shoulder. Her mom and dad smiled and waved again. Angie held up a finger as if to say, 'Wait a minute' and stepped inside.

"Okay," she said as she ripped off the paper. "Mad Libs!" I bought her five new Mad Lib tablets. She was crazy about Mad Libs, and we would play them and laugh until our sides ached. "Thanks, Rachel!" she hugged me and started reading the topics. "These are great! Now open yours."

It was in one of those little gift bags. I reached through the tissue paper and pulled out a pink soap dish. Hmmm, that's kind of strange. "Keep going," grinned Angie. In the bottom of the bag my hand clutched an odd-shape. I pulled it out. Rubber ducky! It was a yellow rubber ducky, like Ernie's, on Sesame Street. Now before you get the wrong idea, remember that Angie and I have been friends since we were little, and we used to love watching Sesame Street together. Well, our favorite episode was the Christmas special (which we have on video) where Ernie trades his rubber ducky to get a cigar box for Bert's paper clip collection, and Bert trades his paper clip collection to get a soap dish for Ernie's rubber ducky! It was just like *The Gift of the Magi*, and Angie and I loved it. So, last year for Christmas I had given her a cigar box full of paper clips as a joke. It never occurred to me that she would get me rubber ducky for Christmas!

A horn blew. "Come on, Ang, we're going to be late... Merry Christmas, Rachel," Angie's mom was yelling out the car window. "Tell your mom I said 'Merry Christmas'!"

"Okay! Merry Christmas!" Angie took off down the sidewalk and jumped in the car. Darn! I forgot to tell her about my toe gift!

"Was that Angie? Why didn't she come in?" Mom asked.

"She was in a hurry. We just swapped gifts," I replied sheepishly, holding out my new rubber ducky. When everyone saw this, I would have a lot of explaining to do. But I had to admit – I loved it!

After I finished defending Angie's gift selection, Uncle Erik announced he needed a ride to the airport to pick up his plane. "No!" we all protested. "You just got here!"

He looked at his watch. "Actually," he answered, it's going on eight o'clock, and I really should've gone hours ago." Once Uncle Erik started looking at his watch there was no way to keep him around.

"But you have to open your last present!" I exclaimed.

"You didn't think I was going to leave without doing *that*?" he asked. "Don't worry – I know the drill!"

"It's late enough. We'll open them all, then we'll take Uncle Erik to the airport, and Christmas will have officially ended," Mom suggested. Gee, it had been such a perfect day, and now it was ending.

Josh opened his. A Gators sweatshirt. Jeremy unwrapped another computer game. "Woo hoo!" Both boys jumped up and prepared to head back to the computer, but Mom made them wait. Dad's last gift was some old antique tool – an old plane. He collected old tools and had them on display in his office. Mom always found them on eBay. Mom's gift was from Jeremy – new oven mitts with a picture of the Pillsbury doughboy. I looked at Uncle Erik and he looked at me.

"You first," he said. I opened the small, heavy gift. Two cans of Rotel tomatoes! He grinned widely and said, "If I could've stayed longer we would've made a batch together!" I felt happy and sad at the same time. He picked up his gift from me. It was heavy, too, but not small. He peeled off the wrap slowly. What if he didn't like it? I always had these last minute reservations. What if he noticed all the mistakes?

"Oh, wow, Rache, honey, this is beautiful!" Angie's mom makes a ton of pottery, and she lets Angie and me paint things for ourselves sometimes. She gave me the idea of making a big, colorful salsa bowl to give Uncle Erik and helped me center the letters in the bottom of the bowl: Uncle Erik's Salsa. The colors were bright and bold, and I thought it was beautiful. And now, so did Uncle Erik. He gave me a big hug, and I wished he could stay forever. "I love it, honey, I really do. I'll bring it along next time, and we'll fill it up together, and then empty it! Okay?" I felt like crying. I was relieved and proud and sad.

"Come on," Dad yelled. "Let's get this pilot on his way." We all liked to watch Uncle Erik pre-flight his plane and take-off.

Twenty minutes later Christmas officially ended as Uncle Erik tilted his wings "goodbye" in the bright Christmas moonlight.

Chapter 16 – Adventures with Adam

Rrrrrriiiinnggggg! I hit my alarm clock, but the ringing continued. It was the phone. I heard mom get it, so I rolled over and closed my eyes again. Footsteps. I burrowed under the covers hoping it was for Josh or Jeremy.

"Rachel, telephone..." Mom handed me the phone.

"Hullo," my voice was sleepy. I had a hard time falling asleep last night after all the excitement of Christmas.

"Hi, Rachel! What'd you get for Christmas?" It was Adam Gopnik. We had agreed to meet today to work on our manatee project. I almost forgot.

"Hi, Adam. I got rollerblades and a CD player. And other stuff. What'd you get?"

"A telescope! Wait'll you see it. I was out last night looking at everything. You can look at the craters on the moon. It's almost as though you can reach your hand out and touch them." Adam's enthusiasm was contagious. I remembered the full moon last night and wondered how Uncle Erik's plane would look through a telescope. If you could see the moon craters, surely you could see Uncle Erik smiling and waving, then he wouldn't have to tilt his wings to say goodbye. "Are you ready to go to the spring?"

The spring! I forgot! Mr. Gopnik promised to take us to Blue Spring State Park today so we could research our manatee project. I had already cleared it with Mom and Dad. I looked at the clock. Seven-thirty. No wonder I was so sleepy. But panic did wonders to wake me up. "Yep, I'm almost ready!" I lied. Adam and Mr. Gopnik were picking me up at eight-fifteen.

"Okay, see you soon!" I jumped out of bed and into the shower. An hour later we were heading down the road.

"Dad, do you think it's cold enough?" Most people think Florida is always hot and sunny, but it could get pretty cold in the winter months. And that's why we were heading to Blue Spring today. Blue Spring is a state park on the St. Johns River. There's a big head spring that feeds into the river, and the water actually looks blue. One hundred million gallons of water a *day* flowed from the spring into the river! Florida is full of springs, and the water temperature is always the same – 72 degrees. Seventy-two degrees doesn't seem all that warm until winter, and then it becomes extremely inviting to manatees that depend on warm water to survive. If it's cold enough elsewhere, the manatees head for the springs to keep warm. The St. Johns River could get as cold as fifty degrees. Adam and I had learned all this while we worked our project, so today would be something of a field trip.

Zipped up in my new jacket, I felt sure it was cold enough. "Yes, I'm guessing you'll see a few manatees today," Mr. Gopnik replied. "Did you bring the camera?" Asking Adam whether he brought the camera was like asking Uncle Erik if he brought his plane. Adam didn't go anywhere without his digital camera. If we got some good pictures today, he would download them on his computer and insert them into the project. We had agreed that he would do the bulk of the computer presentation, and I would handle the big display part. We intended to help each other if we needed to, but so far everything was going fine.

We were surprised to see so many cars at the park on the day after Christmas, but the cold weather was practically a guarantee to see manatees. Guarantee. Manatee. There was a good rhyme if I needed to write a poem for the project.

Mr. Gopnik parked, and Adam and I jumped out. He had the camera, and I had a notebook to take down any information that might be useful. We were a pretty good team. I wondered how our classmates were faring with their projects. "Okay, I brought a chair and a book, and this is where I'll be if you need me for anything." Mr. Gopnik settled back in his chair that he had located in the sunniest spot. It *was* a cold day! He wasn't abandoning us. Adam had already told him our plan, and there was no question that we would be safe as we moseyed around the park. I had been there many times and knew my way around.

"Thanks, Dad. Thanks for bringing us. Stay warm!" Adam and I headed up the boardwalk where we could look over and see warmly dressed adventurers canoeing up and down the St. Johns River. "That looks like fun!" he exclaimed. We continued along the boardwalk toward the head spring, passing by the old Thursby house. Branches from the giant old live oaks reached out over the boardwalk creating a tunnel effect. Spanish moss swayed in the cool winter breeze. Under the right circumstances it could appear spooky.

Suddenly a big raccoon lumbered out of the bushes. "Look, Rachel! Look at that! What do you know? It must be the lure of the trash that brought him out!"

I laughed out loud. "What's so alluring about trash?" I asked. Adam laughed, too. It did sound funny.

"I meant," he giggled. "I meant..." He couldn't stop laughing, and for a minute we watched this poor, confused raccoon wander back into the underbrush as we imagined it looking like a dejected K-Mart shopper who just missed the blue light special on trash. "What I meant," he finally managed, "is that raccoons are nocturnal, so it's just strange to see him out here in the light of day." We both took a deep breath as the laughter subsided. Leave it to Adam Gopnik to know the sleeping habits of animals. He was a walking encyclopedia.

Ahead of us we saw a group of people gathered along the edge of the boardwalk. They peered into the water saying, "Look, look there." Adam looked at me and grinned. Manatees! We dashed to where the crowd had gathered. A tall park ranger wearing an official looking green uniform lectured the crowd.

"…and you can see the scars from the boat propellers if you look closely." He was right. There was a mother and her calf, feeding on the plants in the blue water, and even the young manatee was scarred. I thought of the Jimmy Buffett song as everyone looked sad and went, "Ooohhhhhh!" all at the same time. Manatees are extremely vulnerable to boat motors. We learned it was the leading cause of death, presumably because they were unable to hear the motors until it was too late. So now they are on the endangered species list.

The ranger continued, "The young manatees are nursed by their mothers and begin eating aquatic plants when they're around two months old. Y'all are real lucky to be here today on such a cold day. Manatees typically come in to the spring between November and April on the coldest of days, so seeing these rare creatures today is a little Christmas present from Mother Nature." Adam had his camera out and was shooting pictures. He could look at each picture on the screen on the back of his camera to make sure it was a keeper. Some he deleted, some he saved.

We continued exploring and gathering information. Passing the roped off swimming area on such a cold day was easy. Any other time it would be tempting to jump in. "We should get Mrs. Juarez to bring the class here on a field trip!" Adam suggested.

"Actually, the fourth graders come here every year, so you missed your chance by waiting until you were in the fifth grade to move here. You also missed the fifth grade field trip to Stetson University, which isn't too far from here. That's where Mrs. Juarez went to college, and every year she starts off with a unit on geology, so she takes the class to the Gillespie Museum of Minerals at Stetson. I thought it would be boring, but they even have a piece of amber with a mosquito in it, just like in *Jurassic Park*. Amber is formed from pine sap, so this mosquito got stuck in it, then as the sap hardened it turned into amber, and there's this little mosquito right in the middle of it! There's also a room full of dull, boring looking rocks that glow in all these fluorescent shades of blue and orange – I can't remember all the colors – when the tour guide turns off the regular light and turns on these special black lights."

Adam's animated response was so predictable. "Oh, I'll get my dad to take me there. I'll check it out on the Internet. Leave it to Mrs. Juarez to have the best field trips!" He practically danced with enthusiasm at the thought of such a museum. We chattered along about the virtues of Mrs. Juarez and all the specifics I could remember about the museum.

"The tour guide - her name was Holli - threw a huge rock at Kenny and scared him half to death!"

"Pumice! It must've been pumice!" Adam was enchanted.

"Yeah, that was it. Dried up lava from a volcano."

"Yeah, I'll find out the hours, and maybe we can visit it during the break."

At the head spring we saw divers putting on their gear to go into the spring. The temperature seemed to drop as we shivered and watched them. "Come on in, the water's great!" a diver shouted to his friend. They laughed because the 72 degrees water really was warmer than the outside temperature, which had fallen to around 50 degrees.

"Have you ever been diving?" Adam asked.

"No. It looks kind of fun, but breathing underwater, even with all that equipment, just doesn't seem possible."

"That's what 'scuba' stands for — Self Contained Underwater Breathing Apparatus."

"Oh, that's cool. S – c – u – b – a – scuba! So they fill their tanks with oxygen so they can breathe underwater?"

"Actually, it's a combination of oxygen and nitrogen." Adam centered the divers in his lens and took a picture. "Pure oxygen will kill you below depths of twenty feet." Adam amazed everyone with his easy access to facts and figures about every possible subject. Without coming across as a know-it-all he enlightened everyone he talked to.

Adam and I were having fun, but it was cold, we had our information, and we knew his dad had to be minding the cold by now. When we got back to the place we had left him he was gone. "To the Batmobile!" Adam pointed. Sure enough, Mr. Gopnik had relocated to the confines of the car where we found him reading his book. "Soaking up the solar heat, eh Dad?" Adam asked.

"Yes! It really got cold, didn't it? I'm betting you saw plenty of manatees." Adam held up the camera and pressed the 'view' button to show his dad.

"Want to come up and see them in person?" Adam asked.

"Sure, a brisk walk will feel good. I was starting to get sleepy just sitting here reading." So we walked up for one last look before heading back.

On the ride home Adam chattered away to his dad repeating everything he had learned about manatees. I have a good memory, which is why I'm good in school, but Adam didn't just memorize it for the sake of a test – he was really interested. Mr.

Gopnik suggested we all go back in the summer for a cookout and a canoe ride, and I told him all about the visits my family made to the spring.

"When Josh was little, a squirrel jumped on him down near the parking lot, right after we got there. You know that big oak tree that's sort of growing around the palm tree, and it looks like the branch is an arm wrapped around the trunk? Well, we were all standing there looking at it and wondering how it grew that way, and this little squirrel came scurrying down the trunk and just leaped right onto Josh, then sort of bounced off and scampered away. It was hilarious, but Josh was scared to death. After that, we always referred to the "attack squirrels" of Blue Spring!" The trip home seemed much shorter than the ride over that morning.

"Did you have a good time?" Mom asked when I got home.

"Oh, it was great! It was cold, but that's how we got to see the manatees. We were so lucky Mr. Gopnik took us and that it was a cold day. Plus, I got to wear my new jacket!" I pulled some brochures out of the pocket and hung it in the hall closet. "Now

I'm all ready to get to work on the display part of the project. Adam's going to print some of the best pictures for me to use."

"Well, I'm surprised you have such a big homework project during your winter break, but I'm glad you're enjoying it."

The truth was, these school projects were fun for me. School was what I was good at. Every day I could look forward to feeling good about myself for my accomplishments. All my teachers praised me down through the years, and their opinions were very important to me. I would do a bang-up job on this project, and I knew Adam would do his part, too.

That night I started putting ideas together. There were so many ways to approach it. I had tons of information and wanted the project to be outstanding. I had one of those big three-way folded cardboard displays, the kind you use for science fair projects. My plan was to come up with a catchy, but informative display that everyone would want to see. I would include information about the *Save the Manatees* club. Adam was planning to use that little clip from the Jimmy Buffett song in the computer presentation. Too bad it wasn't longer. It would be great to have an entire song about manatees.

I thought about this for a while. Writing song lyrics must be similar to writing a poem. The hard part was coming up with a melody. I tried to concentrate and hum possible melodies, but sounds from the stereo in the family room distracted me. Mom was still playing Christmas music. *Please come home for Christmas, if not for Christmas, for New Year's Eve...* Manatees *did* come to the springs around Christmas time. That's what the park ranger said. *Manatee, guarantee...* I remembered those rhyming words from earlier.

Christmas music continued to permeate my bedroom walls. I heard Mom singing along. *Jingle bell, jingle bell, jingle bell rock...* That was a great tune to sing along to. I remembered singing along with Dad the night we went Christmas shopping. *Manatee, manatee, manatee rock...* That had a nice sound to it. Gee, it made sense to have a manatee song set to Christmas music. It was winter, after all, when they came in to the springs and people could see them up close.

I yawned, a big, gaping yawn. I looked at my clock. Only nine-thirty, but I was suddenly very sleepy. Of course I had been up late the night before, and today was a big day in the fresh air. A good night's sleep would feel great, and then tomorrow I would tackle the big manatee project.

I brushed my teeth and yelled good night to anyone who might be in earshot. I heard Josh and Jeremy playing on the computer and heard a muffled 'G'night, Rachel' from Mom. I climbed under the big, warm comforter, turned off the light, and curled up in a ball on my side. I was so sleepy.

All of a sudden that gnawing feeling struck me in the stomach. Where was Dad? Then I remembered – he was home, stretched out reading on the couch. It would be a good night.

Manatee, manatee, manatee rock... I hummed myself to sleep.

Chapter 17 – Mysterious Music

It was the day before New Year's Eve. I had made great progress on my project, and Adam was coming over with his part of the project so we could compare notes. Mine was big and bulky, so it made sense for him to bring a computer disk and show me what he had done. Dad was busy cleaning the garage, and Josh and Jeremy were helping. Dad always took off work for the week of Christmas and New Year's. He said he had to so he could get the garage organized to put away all the Christmas decorations. Mom was cleaning closets.

"Rachel, wait'll you hear this!" Adam arrived excited and out of breath. He had ridden his bike, and his cheeks were rosy.

"What is it?" I asked. I knew he was including sound effects on his computer presentation. Maybe he retrieved a sound clip from the Internet. Maybe the sound of a manatee, or the sound of a boat motor.

He took out a CD case. "Rachel, remember that Jimmy Buffett song with the lyrics about manatees?" I nodded. "Well, I was going through all of my Dad's Jimmy Buffett CDs thinking I might find some more manatee lyrics. Rachel, you won't believe what I found!"

"What? What is it?" Adam's excitement was contagious. Curiosity was suddenly killing me.

"Just listen," he said. "Listen very carefully." He had removed his jacket and backpack while he had been talking, and now he was putting the CD into my new CD player. I sat down on my bed and waited. Adam pressed a few buttons, then stood very still and expectantly. A guitar strummed, and a man's voice began to speak:

Back toward the turn of the century, Mark Twain took a trip around the world on a steamship and he wrote a book called 'Following the Equator' and the opening page, as a dedication, it says — 'Be good, and you will be lonesome' -which for me, still seems to work in the fabulous eighties...

Mark Twain! The guy who wrote *Tom Sawyer* and *Huck Finn*. Adam must have thought I would like hearing this. I looked at him to smile, but the expression on his face was so intent and serious. He held his finger to his lips. The guitar played on, and the lyrics began...

> *Jason Mason hears the sound, the whistle blows in Congo Town,*
> *And the mail boat's in, mail boat's in...*
> *Brings him things from oh, so far! Old magazines and Snicker bar,*
> *A simple man, A simple land,*
> *The world's too big to understand,*
> *Be good, and you will be lonesome,*
> *Be lonesome and you will be free,*
> *Live a lie, and you will live to regret it,*
> *That's what livin' is to me, that's what livin' is to me...*

The melody was hauntingly beautiful, the lyrics were mystical and strange. Who was Jason Mason? We had the same last name. Is that why Adam brought it for me to hear? Was it about Mark Twain? Did he write about someone named Jason Mason, like Tom Sawyer or Huck Finn? My mind wandered although I tried to pay attention. I heard the refrain again, the part about living a lie and regretting it. What was this song about? I tried again to listen. The song was ending…

> My **twain** of thought is loosely bound,
>
> I guess it's time to **Mark** this down,
>
> Be good, and you will be lonesome,
>
> Be lonesome and you will be free,
>
> Live a lie, and you will live to regret it,
>
> That's what livin' is to me, that's what livin' is to me…

As the song ended and the guitar strummed again, the singer gently spoke, "*Thank you, Mark.*"

Adam just stared at me. "I don't get it," I said. I was at a loss for words. The song was beautiful, and it was a striking coincidence in several ways. Is that why Adam brought it over? "What did he mean by all that?"

Adam shook his head. "I don't know, Rachel. At first when I heard him talking about Mark Twain, it made me think of you because you like him as an author. Then, the part about Jason Mason was just too weird! I listened to it six times to see if there were any other connections; then I just got the idea to play it for you and see if you could figure it out."

"Well, *I* can't figure it out. I never heard it before, and I don't think I'm related to anybody named Jason. We have Josh and Jeremy in our family. I wonder if Mom and Dad ever considered 'Jason' for a boy's name. Probably not." It was kind of exciting in a way. Coincidences have always fascinated me, but it was Adam who had noticed this one. "Can we play it again?"

He hit the 'repeat' button and we both listened intently. This time I paid closer attention.

On a timeless beach in Hispanola, young girl sips a diet cola,

She's worlds apart, worlds apart,

The spirit of the black king still reverberates through Haitian hills,

He rules the sea, and all the fish,

What if he had a TV dish?

The song was truly beautiful, but had nothing to do with me. Well, Snickers probably counted. That's what Mom put in my stocking every year. The foreign legion, TV dishes, the walrus... nothing made sense. The refrain troubled me. The part about being good and being lonesome was a joke, at least I thought that's what Mark Twain must have meant. For instance, the kids in school who are always clowning around and getting into trouble always have an entourage encouraging them. The well-behaved kids can come across as kind of boring. The troubling part was when he sang, "Live a lie, and you will live to regret it." Those words made me squirm inside. It disturbed me to feel uncomfortable listening to such an otherwise beautiful song.

Adam beamed. "So, what do you think?"

"It's cool. I wonder who Jason Mason is."

"I don't know. I asked my dad if he knew anything about it. The only thing he could tell me is that Jimmy Buffett sings a couple songs that refer to Mark Twain. Anyway, I was just trying to find another manatee song. Wanna see the presentation?"

We changed gears. Jason Mason was forgotten as Adam inserted the disk into the computer in the family room. "Check this out..." A voice, Adam's voice, actually, came out of the speakers: "Manatees – gentle creatures that once roamed Florida's waterways – now extinct!" Wow! It really got my attention! He had done the entire presentation in the future tense, talking about manatees as though they were extinct. "And so, despite legislation and attempts to restrict speeding boats, the last of the manatees died in captivity at Sea World."

I couldn't believe it. On the computer screen, Adam himself appeared as a newscaster reading the evening's news report. What an attention-getter! He gave a comprehensive report about what manatees were like and speculated that perhaps they had not evolved sufficiently to keep up with the modern world that included propellers on boat motors! The picture of Adam faded and was replaced by the shots he had taken at Blue Spring. In between the photos he inserted text that said, "We miss them!" The lines from the Jimmy Buffett song played... *Sometimes I see me, as an old manatee, headin' south as the waters grow colder...* It was very sad and made me think about what it would be like if all the manatees suddenly were gone.

When it ended, he clicked the mouse a few times and demonstrated a computer game he had made. It consisted of questions regarding manatee facts. If the player clicked the right answer, you heard applause. If the wrong answer was selected, a buzzer sounded and Adam's voice said, "Try again." The last question asked was in what year did manatees become extinct.

"Of course, no one can predict the future," Adam was saying, "but my point is that if we don't think about the future and *try* to predict it, we might be facing the loss of something wonderful we took for granted." He had a point. "Since you were focusing on preservation, I decided I should focus on the other aspect of extinction. Don't you think it's a good balance?"

"Yeah, I think it's perfect. Mrs. Juarez will love it!" I was so glad Adam was my partner. He was smart and creative and was willing to work hard. Believe me, there are plenty of kids in our class who were strictly slackers, and it was no fun to be paired with any of them on any kind of project.

I proudly showed Adam my part of the project. I had used the tri-folded project board to create a learning center that emphasized manatee protection. We could set it up in the classroom, and when kids were finished with their work and had some spare time they could do the activities at the manatee center. It was titled "Manatee Preservation: What Can YOU Do?" Under the word "you" I had glued a little mirror so kids could see their faces.

I had included information from the *Save the Manatees* club about how to get involved. Mrs. Juarez always made great learning centers, so I modeled mine on hers. There were several activities for kids to do. One activity was to make a bumper sticker to put on their cars. I had cut strips of white Contact paper into bumper sticker size pieces. I had some permanent markers in a little sleeve attached to the board. My sample bumper sticker said, "I brake for manatees" and was stuck on the board, but kids could write anything they wanted as long as it was a message meant to help protect the manatees. I had listed criteria, just like Mrs. Juarez always did. Another activity was to write a letter to our state legislators to ask them what they were doing to help protect the manatees. I included a sample letter, addresses, and provided stationery.

There was also a word search that included words related to manatees and preservation, and I had drawn a maze shaped like a manatee. There was a boat at one end and some sea grass at the other end so it was as though you were trying to get *away* from the boat and get *to* the grass. I would have to photocopy these at Dad's office or ask Mrs. Juarez to laminate one of each to use at the center. Then kids could use regular markers to circle the words and do the maze and just wipe off the ink when they were done. That was the only part I had to finish.

But the best part was the song. Mrs. Juarez usually included music with her centers, so I did too. I had my old cassette player and headphones to place beside the display board and I included directions for how to use them. I also included words to the song I had finally written. My mom helped me with this part. She had played the music on the guitar and sang the words I wrote, and I recorded it. I couldn't get the tune for *Jingle Bell Rock* out of my head, so I wrote a new set of words and called it *Manatee Rock*. The first verse goes:

Manatee, manatee, manatee rock,

Here's what we'd say if we could talk,

All of you boaters, we wish you'd slow down,

When you come through our river town,

Manatee, manatee, manatee rock,

That's where we hide or under a dock,

We hide from you boaters who drive much too fast,

And that's how we last!

Then the chorus:

There's a fast one, and that's no fun,

Because we swim so slow,

It's a tough dive, just to stay alive,

When we have to go below.

Come on, you manatees, pick up your speed,

Swim on around the dock,

Splashin' and swimmin' in the Florida heat,

That's the manatee rock!

Then the second verse:

Manatee, manatee, manatee rock,

Your boat's on the run, but we wish it would walk,

Your spinning propellers cut us and scar,

Make us look like we've been to war,

Manatee, manatee, manatee rock,

Here's what we'd say if we could talk,

Your boats hurt and kill us and could make us extinct,

How we wish you'd just think!

Then the chorus was repeated, just like in the format of *Jingle Bell Rock*. I had pressed the Play button and watched Adam's face as he listened and followed along with the song sheet. I started to worry like I always did. Maybe it was stupid and geeky. Maybe I shouldn't have had my mom singing. Why did I even try to include music? Why couldn't I have found a cool Jimmy Buffett song like Adam did? Why did I always have to be different?

I was feeling sick in my stomach with apprehension when it finally ended. I looked at Adam.

"Rachel, that's amazing! Did your mom help you write the lyrics?"

"No, I just followed the original song and wrote it like a poem," I said, pointing to the song sheet that said 'Lyrics by Rachel Mason'.

"I'm just totally amazed! And your mom is so talented, too! It must really run in your family. I'm just glad Mrs. Juarez put me with such a creative partner! I hate it when I get stuck with someone who just doesn't care about the assignment!"

Wow! That's exactly what I had been thinking! Now I could hardly wait for school to resume in just a few days. The winter break had been perfect, and now I was anxious to get back to the routine of school and show everyone the great project Adam and I had made.

That night before going to bed I listened to the CD Adam had loaned to me. I wanted to play it for Mom and Dad and Josh and Jeremy, but a part of me wanted to keep it to myself for a little while. I pressed Play and turned the volume down a few notches. The lyrics were printed inside, so I read along as Jimmy Buffett sang. *Live a lie, and you will live to regret it, that's what livin' is to me, that's what livin' is to me...* What a great song.

I went to bed that night humming to myself. *Rachel Mason hears the sound, the whistle blows in Congo Town...*

C hapter 18 – New Year's Day

New Year's Eve and New Year's Day were remarkably uneventful. That was a relief in some ways. Because of my dad's problem when he drank, I always worried about holidays like New Year's when there was so much emphasis on drinking.

But things had been going great at our house, and maybe Dad really *had* stopped drinking for good. I didn't dwell on it but focused instead on my project. I had to refrain from making any significant last minute changes on it and run the risk of messing something up. I set it in the living room so everything would be ready in the morning when we went back to school. Mom was going to drive me so I wouldn't have to defend it on the school bus from curious second-graders.

The Gators were playing today, and that's all Josh, Jeremy and Dad could talk about. They were going to the grocery store to buy soda and snacks. "Too bad we couldn't get Uncle Erik to fly in and whip up some salsa," Dad said, winking at me. "Too bad we don't have his secret recipe!"

Dad was hinting at me to make salsa! It hadn't even occurred to me. "Oh, Dad! *I'll* make salsa!" I was so excited. "You'll have to give me the money to buy the ingredients, though. Otherwise you might guess the secret recipe!"

"It's a deal!" I rode out to the store with Dad and the boys. He gave me a twenty-dollar bill and asked if that was enough.

"Well…" I teased him, "I guess so. But the secret ingredient *is* kind of expensive!" I bought all the ingredients, and Dad bought the corn chips with the other snacks. I checked out and waited up front for them. When we got home, I took over the kitchen and put up a "Keep Out" sign.

Dad, Mom, Josh, and Jeremy tuned in the game. As they cheered and groaned and called advice to the coaches and players, I cut and diced and cut and diced. It took a *long* time to make Uncle Erik's recipe. But it was starting to look and smell like my favorite food. I finally stirred in the last of the diced garlic, scooped out a taste, and knew it was a success!

"Anyone for salsa?" I called out, carrying a bowlful into the family room.

"All right!"

"Finally!"

"Mmmmm, that smells good, Rache, honey!"

I set it down and Mom helped me carry in individual bowls and the chips. Crunching and lip-smacking drowned out the TV announcer.

"This is *great*! Josh said. "Just like Uncle Erik's!" It really was! I didn't want to eat any other snacks, only salsa. I was so proud of myself, and proud that Uncle Erik had given me the recipe. I wished he was there to see what a good job I had done, but he was no doubt off on a flight somewhere.

It was a perfect start to a new year. Tomorrow I would be setting up my learning center and Adam would be demonstrating his computer presentation. He planned to take his dad's laptop to school. I was curious about the other presentations and felt confident that ours would be the best.

That night I was too excited to sleep. I tossed and turned thinking about the manatee song, worrying if the kids would laugh. Then I thought about the salsa and how good it turned out. The next time we had a class party I would volunteer to make a batch. January first. The year was off to a good start.

January first! I could finally write in my new diary! I had almost forgotten. I jumped out of bed and went over to my desk where it had laid since Christmas Day, just waiting for the first of the year. I opened its stiff cover and held it open with one hand while writing with my new gel pen.

January 1 - Today I made salsa! Uncle Erik gave me the recipe for Christmas. It was my toe gift. That sounded kind of dumb, but usually I was a pretty good writer. Well, it's my diary, so I guess it doesn't matter how I write things. *I have my manatee project ready for school tomorrow. Happy New Year!*

It wasn't much of a diary entry, but I never had a diary before. I locked it with its little key and went back to bed. I had better get some sleep. Tomorrow would be a big day.

The Jimmy Buffett song ran through my head again. *Rachel Mason hears the sound, the whistle blows in Congo Town...* I could write new words – words that made sense for Rachel Mason. *Rachel Mason hears the* *sound, the whistle says she's out of bounds...*I giggled. I must be getting sleepy. I had the Gators football game mixed up in my song. *Rachel Mason hears the sound...*

I *did* hear a sound. What was it? Sleepily, I opened my eyes and rolled over to listen. Was I awake or dreaming? Awake. I didn't hear anything after all. I must have been dreaming. Drifting back to sleep I heard the sound again. Footsteps. Running. No, oh no...

C

hapter 19 – Night Sounds

Something crashed and someone yelled. Muffled cries. Voices. I was wide awake now, and hurried out into the hall. I saw Josh standing in the doorway to the living room. He didn't see me approaching but stood transfixed, watching. It felt like a dream. If only it were.

"Mike, *please*…" my mother cried. My steps slowed. I could barely move, but somehow continued toward my brother and the sound of my mother's voice.

"You don't know how hard it is! You think it's *easy*? *Huh*? You think it's easy…" my dad's slurred voice trailed off. *Craaaaccckk!* I heard my mother's sharp intake of breath, heard her sob. *Rachel Mason hears the sound, her father knocks her mother down…* No, no, don't sing that song. Don't hit my mom.

Josh clung to the wall. He looked like a statue of a little boy. Josh, the big brother, was really just a little boy. Something fell and crashed. So many sounds at once. Crying, cursing, crashing. *Rachel Mason hears the sound...*

Josh finally looked over and saw me. He looked past me and I turned and followed his gaze. Jeremy was standing in the dark, quiet and terrified. The three of us huddled and watched our father hit our mother, heard her beg him to stop. We were helpless to do anything but cry silently and hope, hope, hope. Hope that he would stop. Hope that she wouldn't be hurt. Hope that it was just a dream, just a very bad dream.

"Mike, please don't..." she begged again. There was blood on her mouth. I couldn't breathe, couldn't move. My heart pounded, my stomach lurched, and hot tears ran into my mouth. We wanted to stop it, but didn't know how. My mother crouched behind a chair as my dad ranted. He lunged at her and she fled, but even though he was drunk, he was fast and strong and easily grabbed her wrist, wrenching her arm and making her scream in pain.

"Oh, please, God, Mike, stop, please!" She twisted away from him and fell as she tried to get away. He lost his balance and staggered sideways, his foot crashing down on my little tape recorder. My project! I had left my project here in the living room, and now my dad had crushed the tape recorder, lost his balance, and fallen on my learning center display, twisting and bending it.

Oh, this was awful! My project was ruined. Guilt flooded through my mind. How could I even care about my project when my dad was beating up my mom? I cried harder as I watched my dad pick himself up off the floor. He was trying to straighten my project but was only making it worse. "Ohhh, Rache, honey, I'm soooorrry..." he said, realizing what he had done. "I didn't mean to..." I couldn't tell what he mumbled. My project was ruined, and the only good thing to come of it was it had kind of snapped him to attention and distracted him from fighting. He looked around with a shocked look on his face. Shock and dismay, as though someone else had done this. Confusion, as though he wondered how he was unable to prevent it. Now the remorse would begin as my dad would cry and say how sorry he was and how he would never drink again, and my mom would go into the bedroom and cry. Josh,

Jeremy and I would disappear to our own rooms and hide as well, ashamed and unbelieving that our dad had done these awful things.

I was devastated. My stomach was sick, and my head was light. While my mother quietly sobbed in her room, I sat frozen on my bed, hot tears running down my face and neck. I swallowed and tasted salt. How could he do this? How could he be so good to us, and then for no good reason go somewhere and get drunk and beat up our mother? Would he ever stop? He always said he would, that this was the last time, that he was so sorry, that he loved her so much. But this had been going on all our lives. Maybe he could never stop.

And my project. New tears streamed down my face. Tears of shame and fear. Tomorrow was the first day back to school and we were all turning in our projects, but I didn't have one now. What would I tell Adam? And Mrs. Juarez? I could never tell the truth. I never wanted anyone to know about this. What could I do? Maybe I could skip school tomorrow. I could say I was sick. I could make another project. I could tell Adam I had thought of a better idea. I *could* think of a better idea. I looked at the clock. Three-fifteen.

My doorknob turned. "Rachel?" It was Josh. He was carrying my smashed tape recorder. Jeremy was behind him with my display board. It looked even worse than I remembered.

I just stared at them. This was something we didn't do. We didn't talk after the fights, just went to our own rooms and never talked about it, not even the next day or a week later. We simply never talked about it afterwards. But here were my brothers in my room with the pieces of my project.

Josh said simply, "We can help you fix it." I didn't see how, but I also knew that none of us would sleep tonight. By now, Dad was passed out on the couch sleeping, and Mom wouldn't face us until it was time to go to school. "I have an old science project board in my closet. We can just cover everything on it and it'll be as good as new."

"And the tape's okay, Rachel." Jeremy had retrieved the cassette tape of *Manatee Rock* from the tape player. He was right. It was fine. "Maybe your teacher will let you use her tape player." Jeremy was right. Mrs. Juarez would loan me hers.

We began to work methodically and mechanically. We spoke only when necessary, each of us lost in thought, almost grateful for the distraction. Busily and frantically we cut and pasted and remodeled, occasionally whispering requests or directions, but never truly conversing. I looked over at Josh who was deftly covering his old project. The board was in perfect shape, and his cover was looking like a background. Josh the procrastinator. That's what we always called him because he put everything off until the last minute. Maybe this was why. Maybe the last minute was the safest time to do something. I thought of all the hours I had put into my project, then I felt badly when I thought about my mom.

Should we go to her? Should we try to comfort her? We never did, and many times I would wonder what we should be doing. But we all felt ashamed when Dad hit her and couldn't seem to look each other in the eye until some time had elapsed. Tonight was different. There had never been a night like tonight, where Josh and Jeremy and I talked afterwards. But we didn't talk about the fight. We only worked on salvaging my project.

Chapter 20 – Moment of Truth

By six o'clock we were done, and amazingly it was even better than the original display. We were exhausted, and looked it, but I was greatly relieved and thankful to my brothers. I would look for ways to repay them in the future. Like so many mornings in the past, Mom quietly emerged from her bedroom, her face swollen and bruised. I didn't want her to drive me to school. I didn't want anyone to see her. "I can ride the bus, Mom. Jeremy will help me." Jeremy nodded, and Mom looked relieved. No one had an appetite, so no one minded skipping breakfast. We could hear Dad getting ready for work. Somehow he always managed to go to work.

On the bus, kids were talking about what they got for Christmas or where they went for vacation. "Why are your eyes all puffed up?" Haley asked suspiciously.

"The project," I pretended to complain, tilting my head in the direction of the big display board seated next to me on the bus. "I decided to do a bunch of last minute changes and stayed up half the night." I yawned convincingly, because I truly was tired. "My eyes feel terrible!" There, that should do it.

"Yeah, you're such an overachiever! Hey, did you hear about Janelle and Michelle?" Haley's change of subject was a tremendous relief as she launched into some trivial gossip about Janelle and Michelle getting their own phone lines at home.

At school, Mrs. Juarez greeted everyone and buzzed around oohing and aahinng about the projects. "I can't wait to get started!" she exclaimed. "You all must have worked your entire vacation! Now I feel guilty," she joked. It was great to be back to the routine of school. As soon as DEAR time ended Mrs. Juarez announced we would begin our presentations. I had already explained to Adam that I had made a few improvements. He was impressed, I could tell.

When it was finally our turn, we walked confidently to the front of the class. Adam had borrowed a special projector from the media center, so he was able to project the computer presentation onto the overhead screen. The entire class went crazy for his futuristic newscast, and then he called on a few students to come up and answer some of the questions. Kenny answered correctly, and everyone applauded when they heard the applause on the computer. Haley missed hers, and everyone laughed when the buzzer sounded. Adam had done a great job with the sound effects, and the song clip went perfectly with our pictures from Blue Spring. Adam had included one I hadn't seen before. It was a picture of me standing beside a sign at Blue Spring: "Take Only Pictures. Leave Only Footprints." Everyone clapped and cheered, and then Adam made his statement about predicting the future.

"So, to help predict the future of the manatee, Rachel will tell how you can help."

I explained all the activities and described the purpose of the *Save the Manatee* club, and I could tell that everyone was eager to begin. When I finally got to the part about the song, Adam joined me. We had borrowed Mrs. Juarez's tape player. "Well, probably all of you know the song, *Jingle Bell Rock*, so this song, *Manatee Rock* will sound familiar because it's the same melody. But the words are different, thanks to our songwriter, Rachel Mason!" He hit the Play button, nudged the volume control and said, "Enjoy!"

I had never been so nervous! I was tired and jittery anyway, and now I was afraid the kids would laugh. Laugh at me, or worse, at my mother. But no one laughed. They listened. And smiled. As my mom's voice sang, "*Because we swim so slow*" Adam made swimming motions with his arms. "*It's a tough dive, just to stay alive,*" and there was Adam pretending to dive, "*when we have to go below...*" and with this line he held his nose and wiggled down towards the floor. He continued to act out parts of the song, and the entire class was enthralled, especially Mrs. Juarez who tapped her foot and shook her head back and forth to the rhythm of the song. By the time it ended, everyone had picked up the simplest part and sang together loudly, "*That's the manatee, that's the manatee, that's the manatee rooooooooock!*"

We did it! It was over, and it was a success. I loved my brothers and owed them a gigantic debt. "Great job, Rachel!" Adam whispered as we took our seats. "I'm really sorry about your tape player." I had told him I dropped it on the way to the bus stop that morning. I hated to lie, but it's something I had learned to do at times.

"Yeah, I'm just glad it's over and nothing went wrong!"

Later that day Mrs. Juarez talked to Adam and me together. "I'm really proud of you two, and quite impressed! Adam, I know you love computers, but I had no idea of your level of expertise! And Rachel, at the beginning of the school year when you told me you wanted to be a teacher, well, I just have to tell you that your learning center far surpasses anything I've ever done." This wasn't really true, but I could practically feel my head swell. "When I need some technical assistance, I will certainly be asking for your help, Adam." Adam seemed to puff up at all these compliments. "And Rachel, when you get to middle school next year, I hope you'll consider joining the FFEA – Florida Future Educators Association."

My head was just spinning. I was so happy. Mrs. Juarez said a lot of other nice things - that my mother did such a great job on the song and what a good songwriter I was. She asked if I had a favorite songwriter. I had never even considered anything other than favorite authors, but without hesitating I smiled at Adam and blurted out, "Jimmy Buffett!"

The bus ride home that day wasn't all that bad despite my worrying about my parents. I always wondered and worried about the state of things, although I had an idea of what to expect. Today I only wanted to think about how well our project had turned out. Mrs. Juarez said it looked like I had spent weeks on my project, which just goes to show you that even though teachers are smart, they're not *that* smart. Josh, Jeremy, and I had only worked about three hours on the project, and no one would ever know.

It was quiet when Jeremy and I walked into the house. Mom had rearranged everything in the living room. She did that sometimes after a fight. I think it was her way of camouflaging whatever got broke. Or maybe she just wanted a change of scenery. Dad wasn't home, and there was no sign of Mom. I dropped my backpack and tiptoed through the house. Maybe she was napping. No. Her bedroom door was open, but she wasn't there. I felt like I would throw up. Maybe they fought again this morning after we left for school. Maybe she had finally had enough and left.

Jeremy was looking, too. "She's in the back yard, Rachel." I looked out the window and saw Mom filling up the birdfeeder. A giant sigh of relief escaped my lungs. I didn't even realize I had been holding my breath. That was just like Mom to go on like everything was normal. And just like all the other times, I guess this really was normal.

Dad came home from work on time, and although conversation was strained, we all pretended it had never happened. Except for the bruise on Mom's face, it might not have happened at all. Josh was telling a funny story about one of his teachers getting into an argument with another student about who really discovered America. I half listened and thought about my day in school, but I couldn't really talk about it without mentioning the project, and that would bring last night into the conversation.

"Oh, Uncle Erik called today," Mom said. "He'll be up this way next weekend and wants to know if anyone is ready for a flying lesson." We all clamored and inquired for details. Anytime Uncle Erik was mentioned you had our undivided attention. "I told him about your salsa, Rachel, and he said to tell you to save him some."

The day had turned out alright, even if I didn't have breakfast, even if I did have to lie to Haley about my red, puffy eyes and to Adam about my tape player, even if my dad had beat up my mom the night before. Things weren't really so bad. I finished my homework, math and spelling, and called Angie to tell her all about how great our presentation had gone.

"You're so lucky to have Mrs. Juarez. Old Misery didn't even ask us how our vacation was. She just started right in on us about how far behind we are!" We talked until it was time for bed.

I listened to the Jimmy Buffett song again. One of these days, after everything was really back to normal, I would play it for my family. I knew they would get a kick out of it. Maybe we even had a relative named Jason Mason. Maybe it would be something like Adam Gopnik, the writer, and Adam Gopnik, my friend. I listened to the melody and the words I now knew by heart... *Be good, and you will be lonesome, Be lonesome and you will be free, Live a lie, and you will live to regret it, that's what livin' is to me, that's what livin' is to me...* I wondered if Jimmy Buffett had lived a lie. Or Mark Twain. Or Jason Mason. I wondered who had lived a lie.

As I got ready for bed, I thought about the lies I told that day. Sometimes a lie is all we have when the truth is too ugly to tell. I remembered other lies, like telling Mrs. Juarez about my great breakfast that day we started our nutrition unit. These were the kinds of lies I told. I wondered if telling a lie was the same as living a lie, or if living a lie felt worse. Maybe there was no difference. Telling lies was bad enough, especially when the reason you told the lies was because you were ashamed of someone you loved. I didn't want to be ashamed of my dad, or my mom. I wished my dad would quit drinking and we could have a nice, normal family, like the Benningstons or Angie's family. But deep inside, I knew I could never change my dad or anyone else. I could only be me – Rachel Mason – and maybe I couldn't even change myself.

I climbed under the covers and thought about Uncle Erik and wondered if he knew the truth about my dad. I wondered if I could ever be brave enough to talk to him about it. I imagined what that conversation might be like. Would he be shocked? Would he say something like, "Oh, Rachel, why didn't you tell me sooner? All we have to do is…" and then Uncle Erik would tell me the secret of how to get my dad to quit drinking. A secret even better than the salsa recipe.

I took a deep breath and rolled over. My mind zipped around on so many subjects, and a part of me always dreaded going off to sleep, dreaded what sounds might wake me in the middle of the night, like last night. Maybe Uncle Erik *would* know what to do. Maybe he could get my dad to change. They were brothers, after all. Maybe I *should* talk to Uncle Erik the next time I saw him. I am the eternal optimist, always hopeful for a happy ending, even if I have to make it up myself.

Just then I remembered my diary. It was only the second day of this new year, and already so much had happened. Too much. I got back out of bed, turned on the light, and unlocked it with the little key. I re-read my first entry as I tapped the pen on the edge of its pages. My mind replayed the events of the last 24 hours... the fight, staying up all night with Josh and Jeremy, trying to explain my puffy eyes, and of course, our presentation. Finally I wrote:

January 2 – What a great day! Mom rearranged the living room – it looks wonderful! Our manatee presentation was awesome. Everyone loved my song, and Adam acted out parts like he was diving or swimming. I'm glad I spent so much time on my project. Mrs. Juarez said I'm going to be a great teacher someday! Uncle Erik called to say he is coming to visit. It will be great to see him again. We have so much to talk about...

The End

Predict the Future

Rachel doesn't exactly lie in her diary entry, but she certainly leaves out details. If nothing changes, imagine how her life will be in the future – 5 years, 10 years, 20 years. Now, imagine how her life might change if Uncle Erik or someone else is able to intervene and help. Her life will likely take a different direction entirely. Readers of *Rachel Mason Hears the Sound* are invited to predict Rachel's future by logging on to www.rachelmason.com and creating a diary entry for some future date. You can read other diary entries there, too.

Dear Diary,

_____

_____

_____

_____

_____

_____

_____

_____

_____

_____

Rachel Mason

Help and Hope

Log on to www.rachelmason.com for useful information and the most current list of organizations that might help Rachel and others like her.

Al-Anon/Alateen: Is Your Life Affected by Someone's Drinking?
http://www.al-anon.alateen.org/
1-888-425-2666

Effects of Domestic Violence on Children and Adolescents: An Overview
http://www.aaets.org/arts/art8.htm

Helping Kids Navigate Their Teenage Years: When Parents Need Help First
http://www.4therapy.com/consumer/conditions/item.php?uniqueid=6261&categoryid=240&

The Effects of Domestic Violence on Children
http://www.aifs.gov.au/nch/issues2.html#effect

About the Author

Cindy Lovell Oliver dropped out of high school in the 11th grade despite her dream of becoming a classroom teacher. She began attending college at the age of 35 and eventually fulfilled her life's dream of becoming a 5th grade teacher in Florida. She earned a Ph.D. at the University of Iowa and went on to teach at the college level. Her areas of expertise include gifted education, teaching English as a second language, and Mark Twain. Cindy has two grown children, Angela and Adam. She lives in Florida with her husband, Jim, who is also a teacher.

Cindy can be reached through N.L. Associates for young author and teacher workshops on writing.

NL Associates Inc
PO Box 1199
Hightstown, NJ 08520-0399
732-605-1643
www.storieswithholes.com

Dynamic Speakers
Creative Workshops
Relevant Topics

Nathan Levy, author of the *Stories with Holes* series and *There Are Those*, and other nationally known authors and speakers, can help your school or organization achieve positive results with children. We can work with you to provide a complete in-service package or have one of our presenters lead one of several informative and entertaining workshops.

Workshop Topics Include:
- Practical Activities for Teaching Gifted Children
- Critical Thinking Skills
- Teaching Gifted Children in the Regular Classroom
- How to Read, Write and Think Better
- Using *Stories with Holes* and Other Thinking Activities
- Powerful Strategies to Enhance the Learning of Your Gifted and Highly Capable Students
- Powerful Strategies to Help Your Students With Special Needs be More Successful Learners
- The Principal as an Educational Leader
          And many more…

Other Titles Available from NL Associates, Inc.

Not Just Schoolwork
Volumes 1-4

Write, From the
Beginning
(Revised Edition)

Thinking and Writing
Activities for the Brain!
Books 1 and 2

Creativity Day-by-Day
(Stimulating Activities for
Kids and Adults)

Stories with Holes
Volumes 1-20

Intriguing Questions
Volumes 1-6

Whose Clues
Volumes 1-6

Nathan Levy's
Test Booklet of Basic
Knowledge for Every
American Over 9 Years
Old

There Are Those

101 Things Everyone
Should Know About
Science

Stories with Holes
Gift Set Volumes 1-12
Sample stories taken
from 19 of the 20
original volumes of
Stories with Holes. Some of
the more difficult stories
have been omitted. The
glossy covers make this
set more appropriate as a
gift.

Please write or call to receive our current catalog.
NL Associates, Inc.
PO Box 1199
Hightstown, NJ 08520-0399
(732) 605-1643
www.storieswithholes.com